MIDNIGHT LYNCHING

When Ruby Malone's husband is lynched by a sheriff's posse, Wells Fargo investigator Asa Harker goes after the beautiful widow expecting her to lead him to the vast sum of money stolen from his company. But Ruby has gone on the outlaw trail with the handsome, young Ben Whitman. Worse still, Harker finds he must deal with a crooked sheriff. Without help, it looks as if he will not only fail to recover the stolen money but also lose his life into the bargain.

TERRY MURPHY

MIDNIGHT LYNCHING

Complete and Unabridged

LINFORD
Leicester

First published in Great Britain in 1998 by
Robert Hale Limited
London

First Linford Edition
published 1999
by arrangement with
Robert Hale Limited
London

British Library CIP Data

Murphy, Terry, *1962 –*
    Midnight lynching.—Large print ed.—
    Linford western library
    1. Western stories
    2. Large type books
    I. Title
    823.9'14 [F]

ISBN 0–7089–5433–2

Published by
F. A. Thorpe (Publishing) Ltd.
Anstey, Leicestershire

Set by Words & Graphics Ltd.
Anstey, Leicestershire
Printed and bound in Great Britain by
T. J. International Ltd., Padstow, Cornwall

This book is printed on acid-free paper

1

Most folk reckoned the winter just gone was the coldest ever remembered in Montana. Even the few oldtimers left, the ones who'd had to fight their way west against the Indians, admitted that it had been colder than anything they'd known. Ruby Malone wasn't about to argue with them. It had been tough going for her all alone in the shack up in the mountains by Wheelbreak Pass. A lot of the time she hadn't been able to make the three miles down to Martin Mead's farm. All she could do was wrap herself up in blankets and, still shivering, pray that things wouldn't get worse and she'd run out of victuals. That hadn't been likely to happen. Up there on the top of the range the snowdrifts never got so bad. Anyway, the Meads wouldn't have left her to perish. Pearl would have made sure that Martin or Elias, their hired-man, got to Ruby. Her only income was from the chores she did for them. Ruby knew that they thought of her as a young widow-woman and she was too ashamed to let them know any different. The last she'd heard of Edward, her husband, was when a sheriff and two deputies came riding up last Fall to enquire about him. Soft-spoken but sly-eyed, the sheriff hadn't believed her when she'd said she hadn't seen neither hide nor hair of him for gone two years.

She had no need to lie. It was Edward who was on the wrong side of the law, not her. That was why she now thought one of them was coming back as she stood in the window watching the lone rider come up the trail from the township of Blue Creek. They'd waited out the winter. That figured. Edward Malone had been wanted for a whole mess of robberies, rustling and the like, the last time she had seen him. Doubtless he had added considerably to the list since then.

A pale, late-evening sun and a delayed twilight lied about it being spring. Ruby was so cold that she draped a heavy shawl across her shoulders as she watched and waited. She had her long golden hair twirled up high on her head in the way she had seen a woman wearing hers in an illustrated catalogue down at Hebron's store in Blue Creek.

The new hairstyle enhanced her already striking appearance. Ruby knew that. There wasn't any sense in taking on some kind of foolish modesty. There'd been a time when her Roman nose, high cheekbones and wide mouth had men trailing after her. Up here she kept herself looking as smart as possible. A pointless exercise, perhaps, for all there was to look at her was the occasional deer or mountain lion, both from a distance.

The rider was nearing now. The poor light of the edge of dusk was imparting some kind of menace to the way he sat in the saddle. Giving a nod of self-agreement with something that had gone on inside of her head, Ruby went to the mantelpiece and took down the Henry rifle. Hand going into an already open box of shells, she loaded it.

With the rifle under her arm, she came back to the window. The firearm, which she could use as well as any man, gave her confidence. There had been times when she hadn't a scrap of food in the shack, yet nothing would induce her to get rid of the Henry. A lone woman couldn't take any chances. Even a bright shiny star on a man's breast was no assurance that there wasn't a darkness to his soul. She'd had to fight occasionally; the worse time was when she'd had to use a knife on an amorous trapper. He had gone off, staggering into the night, clutching his lacerated groin, screaming and howling his agony as loud as any grizzly with its leg caught in a steel trap.

A shudder went through her as

she thought for a moment that she recognized the approaching rider. Still unable to see his face, Ruby made a positive identification from the way he sat in the saddle. That was the way she had learned to do this kind of thing. Holding off to get a look at a face made it too late to do anything if whoever it was turned out to be a threat.

Heading towards her at a leisurely pace, like a range-rider returning after a hard day, was Edward Malone, coming home after an absence of long years.

Replacing the rifle above the fireless grate, Ruby came back past the big double bed that was ever a reminder that she had been deserted. Standing just inside of the door, she made no attempt at this stage to lift the thick bar from across it.

Aware that a traumatic time lay just ahead, she welcomed it as a turning point. Tonight, her future would be decided, one way or another. If her husband didn't have something to offer their marriage, then she would leave here to go her own way. Not yet thirty years old, she wasn't prepared to let any more time go by with her isolated up here on the high ground. She needed a proper life, deserved a proper life, and was determined to live one from now on. Some perverse loyalty had prevented her leaving while Edward was away; now he was back she would confront him with an ultimatum.

The steady rhythm of hoofbeats slowed before dying out. Then there came the irregular clumping of the hoofs of a tethered horse. Edward called her name, low and furtively. 'Ruby?'

As she suspected he would, her husband was showing the caution of a hunted man. He couldn't walk up to the shack without being sure that only she was inside. In the past he had slept only fitfully, listening for any suspicious noise. His nervousness had been contagious, putting Ruby on edge.

There were times when she pitied him. Times when she grieved for a husband who was living a life even more insular than her own. For years he had known little more than the empty existence of the frontier saloons and the desperate loneliness of the outlaw trail.

'I'm here,' she said, just loud enough for him to hear.

'Open up, Ruby,' he called.

Using all her strength she lifted off the bar, pausing for a split second to absorb a prophetic feeling that life would change drastically once she opened the door.

Edward came inside in his jerky, fast way. His movements were those of an animal beset by predators. Replacing the door, Ruby turned to face him. He wasn't a big man, but she had been alone for so long that he seemed to fill the shack. Although he was her husband, she found his presence oppressive.

'Ruby!' he said, making her name

into a greeting combined with an unspecific apology.

She said nothing. A few short years had aged him disproportionately. A light that had burned in his eyes had been dimmed to the point of extinction. His face was haggard and, worst of all for Ruby, a boyishness that had always appealed to her had disappeared.

'I'm home,' he said lamely. Although unable to recognize most of his many faults, Edward was ever mindful of his failure as a husband.

Remaining silent, Ruby went anxiously to the window. It was darker now, but as far as she could tell the trail down as far as Wheelbreak Pass was deserted.

'Is there a posse behind you, Edward?'

Coming across the room to place a bulging saddle-bag on the table, he said, 'It isn't like you think, but I am in trouble, Ruby.'

'Sit down,' she said wearily, slipping the shawl from her shoulders. She couldn't recall a time when he hadn't been in some kind of bother. Since being put out of work as a cowboy by the drought of '83, when so many ranches had gone out of business, Edward Malone, in the way of countless other cowboys, had robbed and thieved. She had an egg intended for her breakfast, and a steak Pearl Mead had given her when she had left the farm that afternoon. 'I'll cook you something.'

Edward sat, but he said, 'I don't reckon I'll have time for no chow, Ruby. Has anyone been here for me?'

'There was a sheriff here last Fall,' she told him, noticing his relief to hear that it hadn't been more recently.

He laid his right arm protectively across the saddle-bag on the table in front of him. 'What did he look like?'

Ruby shrugged, raking through her memory. 'I don't recall him too well. He wasn't a big man. Not much taller than me. He talked real quiet, almost a whisper, and carried a scattergun.'

'That's Turps Hallam!' Edward gasped fearfully, glancing at the door as if he expected the sheriff he spoke of to be standing there.

A quick anger rose in Ruby; it dissolved into sorrow. Her errant husband had returned to offer her nothing more than further trouble. Lighting the oil lamp, turning up the wick when it caught, casting dramatic shadows, she said, 'I'll get you that meal.'

'I've come for you, Ruby,' he said, as she heated fat in a pan.

Ruby gave a harsh laugh. 'You've come for me! My God, Edward, it's not much of a life here, but it's sure better than being on the run with you. What will we do, starve until you hit the next bank, or rustle your next herd?'

'It won't be nothing like that, Ruby,' he told her, with an insistence that came close to being convincing. He gave the packed saddle-bag a pat with the hand that was still resting on it. 'There's a fortune in here. We can go anywhere, Arizona, Texas, anywhere you choose, and set ourselves up for life.'

Shaking her head, flipping an egg from the pan to a plate, she answered, 'No, Edward. You stole that money.'

'I didn't steal it, Ruby.'

For some odd reason she believed him, although she couldn't accept that whatever money was swelling the saddle-bag had been come by honestly, so she said, 'If it wasn't you who stole it, then somebody else did.'

She slid the plate on the table in front of him. Edward began to eat swiftly, the way a person on the run did, a person who expected every meal to be interrupted. His hunger was evident, too. Ruby stood back to study him. Once she had gained a womanly satisfaction from feeding her man. All she wanted now was him out of here. Then she would leave, too. Her immediate future was bleak, but it would be worse if she went with Edward. Long ago he had ceased to be a husband and had become a liability.

11

She had learned to put no stock in his fragile dreams.

'That was great,' he complimented her, pushing an empty plate from him, slapping his stomach appreciatively with both hands. 'Get your things together, Ruby, and we'll leave.'

Pulling in a deep breath, she spoke as she exhaled so as to keep her voice firm. 'I am not going with you, Edward.'

Anger brought him half up out of the chair. There was menace in his tone as he reminded her, 'You are my wife, Ruby!'

'That's something I never forgot, but you did,' she replied accusingly.

He stood then, so violently that the chair was knocked over backwards. The nervousness that had agitated him since he'd arrived at the shack appeared to be fuelling his anger. He had never hit Ruby in the past, but it seemed to her that was about to change.

Then her heart skipped a beat and Edward's face drained to a ghastly white as a noise came from outside. Ruby heard it, and knew that the sound didn't fit just the one restless horse. Edward was twisting this way and that, as if preparing to run. But he was confined by the four walls of the shack, and he hissed at her urgently, 'Turn down the lamp.' There was no point in obeying. To dim the lamp now would only serve to increase the suspicions of whoever was outside. They weren't left guessing by the next sound they heard; it was the unmistakable chink of horses' shoes on loose stones.

'Quick, Edward,' Ruby hissed, keenly aware that it was he who had brought someone to the shack. 'Go out the back window and up on to the roof. They won't find you in the dark.'

Dashing to the window, he came back to take the saddle-bag with him. Ruby saw him go out backwards. He could easily reach to the roof and pull himself up.

'This is Deputy-Sheriff Rawlings here,' a deep voice spoke from outside the door. 'You'd best open the door, ma'am — and open up mighty quick!'

Satisfied that Edward was out of sight, Ruby struggled with the heavy bar across the door for the second time that evening. The door opened and a startled Ruby saw five men standing there. Ruby took the one nearest to her to be Rawlings. He had a cruel face in which the dark eyes were slightly crooked. A little behind him was the sheriff who had called on her months ago. He smiled at her friendly-like, as if they were meeting at some social get-together. Remembering that the plate Edward had used was still on the table, Ruby covered it with her folded shawl, hoping that she would be seen to be carrying out a woman's instinctive action of tidying up for visitors.

'We had reason to believe that Edward Malone was here, ma'am,' Hallam said conversationally in his quiet way, looking around him. 'But I guess we were wrong.'

The others were peering round the shack, all looking bored and anxious to be away. They were too easily satisfied, and Ruby wasn't fooled. She said indignantly, 'I haven't seen my husband since you were here last, Sheriff.'

'Seeing as he ain't here, I guess I ain't got no call to doubt your word, Mrs Malone,' Hallam said affably.

'It's just that the horse outside made us kind of curious,' Rawlings explained, given a slyness by his crossed eyes.

'Oh that!' Ruby thought rapidly, trying not to trip over her words. 'That's my horse, well, one the farmer I work for let me borrow for going to and fro. It's a fair old hike.'

'Then I guess the horse comes in mighty handy, ma'am,' Hallam said with an agreeable nod.

But Ruby froze inside as she saw him casually reach out a hand to move a corner of her shawl to reveal the dirty plate. She also noticed that the deputy had his head on one side, listening. Unable to hear anything at first, she then gave an involuntary little cry as there was a sliding, scraping sound overhead. Then came a dull thud just outside the still open door. Heart going cold, she realized that Edward, probably due to the state of his nerves, had slipped off the roof.

The three men in the doorway moved fast. They turned away, there was a scuffle, and when they turned back it was to throw Edward into the shack. He hit the floor hard, rolled on to his back, and was about to get up when Rawlings placed a high-heeled boot on his throat, pinning him to the floor. The saddle-bag was thrown in next, and a smiling sheriff picked it up.

'Nice of you to drop in, Malone,' he said, and there was some sniggering from his men at the joke. 'You sure are an unlucky cuss. If you hadn't fallen off that roof we'd have ridden off to look for you elsewhere.'

When Edward spoke his voice was

16

rasping. 'This ain't none of Ruby's doing, Hallam.'

For the first time in many a year, Ruby felt a warmth for her husband. He was in a dire situation, but he was doing his best to protect her. Hallam was holding his chin thoughtfully as he studied her.

'I reckon as how you could be guilty of a right serious offence, Mrs Malone,' the sheriff said at last, turning his head to Deputy Rawlings. 'What say you on this, Caleb?'

Increasing the pressure of his foot on Edward's throat, Rawlings gave what sounded like a considered opinion. 'The way I see it, Sheriff, the lady didn't have no kind of choice. Now we've got what we came after, it don't seem right to me to bother her any more.'

'Then so be it,' Hallam nodded gravely. 'Get him out of here.'

The trio at the door came in, filling the shack as they bent and pulled Edward up from the floor. As they

17

dragged him toward the door, he turned his head to speak to Ruby.

'I'm sorry, Ruby, for this, and for all the other things, I guess,' he said humbly before they got him outside.

Then Hallam was raising his stetson to her, speaking in his low-pitched voice as he and Rawlings went out of the shack. 'Forgive us for the inconvenience we have incurred, Mrs Malone, and may I bid you goodnight.'

As soon as she was alone, Ruby closed the door and lifted the bar back into place. Even then she couldn't rid herself of a feeling of insecurity. The men coming into her domain — and she felt a stab of guilt as she included Edward with them — had robbed her of some inner privacy. Although unable to define the feeling, Ruby found it to be distressing.

Making herself coffee, she sat at the table drinking it. Try though she did, it was impossible for her to remember Edward sitting there eating a meal so short a time ago. It was as if he and the others had never been there. The sensation this gave was every bit as disturbing as the earlier belief that she had somehow been invaded physically.

Lying in a huge bed that was symbolic of her failed marriage, sleep didn't come for hours. To a background of the partially harmonious cries of nightbirds, she lay awake thinking. Where would they have taken Edward, and what charges would he face? Should she go to see him, or was it better for them both if she made a clean break now? These were problems that needed to be settled immediately, but she had no answer to any of them before exhaustion caught up with her and she slept.

Her head ached when she awoke in the morning. The pain jumbled her thoughts so that she had to lie still to let the events of the previous night slot into order. As her mind cleared, so were all her pre-sleep questions answered in a rush. She knew what she had to do. Edward Malone no longer had any claim on her, and with his tenuous hold over her had gone her virtual imprisonment here in this shack. Looking out of the window she saw, with relief, that Sheriff Hallam had left Edward's horse outside. It stood picketed and forlorn, still saddled. After she got her few belongings together, she would tend the animal so that it was fit for her to ride.

Packing the two spare calico dresses she owned into a satchel, she put on an Eton jacket, took the rifle down from its position above the mantelpiece, and was ready to leave.

Reaching the door she turned to look back into the shack. Not knowing what emotion to expect, she was surprised to feel absolutely nothing. Leaving this shack that had been home meant no more to her than walking away from a public building. Not knowing whether this pleased or saddened her, Ruby closed the door slowly and started toward the horse.

To her amazement the horse, which

had been standing all night saddled, was no longer listless. In fact it was skittish, neighing loudly and shying away from Ruby each time she tried to approach it.

Edward had picketed the animal close to a big stretch of wood that stood close to the north-east corner of the shack, which made Ruby pretty sure of what the trouble was. Laying her bag down on the dawn-moist ground, she brought her rifle level to her waist and stepped quietly to the trees. The big cats didn't usually come this close except when everything was frozen solid and they were starving. But she guessed that a rogue mountain lion was somewhere in there this morning, scaring the horse.

With the rising sun against her, coming blindingly through the trees, she knew that she needed to take care. Although not expecting the cat to attack, she didn't want it to have all the advantages.

That was when she found out that she was wrong. It wasn't a lion that had got the horse into such a state. Going round the massive girth of an ancient tree, she jerked back as her head almost collided with a swinging pair of booted feet.

Only for a moment was she paralysed by fear. Toughened by life out West, hardened by living alone under adverse conditions, Ruby Malone looked up to find herself looking into the eyes that were bulging from the purple face of her husband. Dropping her gaze, fearing that she was about to vomit, she did a stiff-legged walk back to the horse.

She wondered what kind of a sheriff Turps Hallam was. It was now plain that shortly after being taken from the shack, Edward Malone had been lynched.

Speaking softly to the horse, Ruby was able to calm it sufficiently to be able to mount up. Without a backward glance at either the shack or the trees, she headed for Wheelbreak Pass.

2

Rosie Diamond's *parlour house*, the Blue Goose, stood on a hill outside the town limits. She had previously been in business down on the main strip, until the newly formed Bannon town council went on a moral crusade. Rosie's establishment was the first victim.

'We don't want a bordello on a street where our wives and children regularly walk,' John Kramer had declared righteously. The same John Kramer, the local land agent, had sold Rosie Diamond the new property up on Prospect Hill.

Rosie could put up with the hypocrisy, accepting that there was no honest businessman or woman, but there were other reasons for her resentment at being moved. She was doing fairly well. Unlike the smaller, bawdier houses, she provided a spacious lounge for which she had bought a piano and hired a pianist. The six girls she employed were of a reserved nature, closer to being genteel young ladies than the busty, foul-mouthed types usually associated with such a house. The principal disadvantage was one of location. Her place was all uphill from downtown. This deterred many of her short-winded customers, while others were forced to hire a buggy in order to pay a visit. Rosie was seriously considering providing free transport to cater for the weekend rush. A shuttle service between her place and the town could be a winner.

None of this ever crossed the mind of Ben Whitman. Never failing to visit the Blue Goose when he had occasion to be in Bannon, he had become one of Rosie's favourites. Aged just twenty-six and as fit as a fiddle, Whitman as yet had no price on his head, no picture or description of him had been posted. As free as the wind, he liked the exercise of walking up the hill to Rosie's place.

That evening, just as he had on his other visits, Ben left his horse down in the town's River Street livery stable to take a leisurely stroll up the hill.

He made a point of never outstaying his welcome, delaying only long enough to enjoy a drink on the house with Rosie. She engaged him in her customary bland chit-chat, neither wanting to know anything about her clients nor have them learn anything about her. There were men of all types in already. Not far from where Whitman sat with Rosie, a game of chuck-a-luck was in progress. He found the fast, insistent rattle as the three dice were thrown to be an annoying distraction. Chinese house-boys wearing permanent smiles, moved around as silently as phantoms.

Whitman had a question that had been building in him for more than an hour. When he had walked up to the Blue Goose that evening, the most magnificent specimen of womanhood he had ever seen had been standing outside. A lowering sun had brushed a magic into the golden hair that fell nearly to her waist. She held her head in a proud way to accentuate features that, though strong, were femininely lovely. The Eton jacket she wore was short enough to show off the erotic swell of her hips. Ben Whitman was a ladies' man, but he had never before seen a lady like that.

Desperately wanting to ask Rosie if she knew who the woman was, Whitman knew better than to give way to his curiosity. The strangest thing of all was that the mystery woman had been carrying a Henry rifle. At first, he had suspected that she was some wronged wife waiting to deal with a philandering husband when he came out of the Blue Goose.

But, a good judge of people, Whitman had changed his mind. There was no anger to the woman. What did become plain to him was the air of poverty that even her beauty and proud manner could not conceal. Though not badly worn, her clothes had a recently acquired shabbiness. He gained the impression that she had been sleeping out under the stars. When the probable truth came to him it was a shock. All the signs said times were so bad for her that she was trying to find the courage to enter the Blue Goose and apply for work.

With no qualifications as a moralist, quite the opposite in fact, Ben Whitman considered there to be an off-beat blasphemy to the prospect of such a woman taking even a single step inside of this place.

But he discovered that was what she was about to do as he came face to face with her on his way out. Blocking her way, rudely forcing her back a little so that Rosie Diamond couldn't see what was taking place, Whitman said, 'This isn't no fit place for a lady, ma'am.'

Expecting her to resent being prevented from entering, he discovered that her resolve was so weak that he was intimidating her.

'But . . . ' she began, her voice trailing away because she could think of nothing to say.

Encouraged by her meekness, Whitman took her by an elbow and moved her out through the door. They walked a few short steps together. Lights were being lit in the town down below. It was a scene which held them in the uneasy half-world in which a day dies.

'I can't let you go in there,' he told her.

'What is it to you?' she enquired, puzzled rather than angered by his interference.

'Nothing . . . everything . . . I mean . . . ' he stammered, for the first time in his life being unable to find words.

'You know why I was going in, don't you?'

The ashamed way that she said this to a stranger was as ludicrous as his concern for her. Her frown did nothing to mar her loveliness.

Bewilderment added depth to the

large blue eyes with which she was studying him.

'I guess that I do,' he nodded, 'and the Blue Goose is no fit place for a lady like you.'

'A lady like me!' she repeated, a trace of harsh amusement in her voice. 'This *lady*, mister, hasn't eaten for two days. I sold my horse more than a week ago, and last night I slept out back of the Kicking Bear saloon. So I need to be in there. Please stand aside.'

Obstinately standing in her way, Whitman said, with a touch of disgust; 'And now you are prepared to sell yourself?'

'I have nothing else,' she told him wearily, devoid of self-pity.

'Why don't you sell that?' He pointed at the Henry rifle.

'Never.' She breathed the word out like a sigh, looking affectionately at the firearm.

'Can you use it?'

'I can use it, mister,' she told Whitman, with a quiet confidence.

After a moment's pondering, he gave an emphatic nod before saying, 'Then you've no need to go in there. Come on back down to town. I'll buy you a meal.'

He had already moved off in the direction of Bannon, but she stood still, looking after him with suspicion.

'Why would you want to do that?' she called.

Pausing, he turned to face her. She was back-lit by the last rays of a setting sun. Complete with a golden halo she could have been an angel. But Ben Whitman knew that if angels did exist, then they never came this far West.

'I'm thinking of offering you a partnership,' he replied, his words coming as a surprise to him as well as her.

'Doing what?'

She had begun to follow him, slowly and cautiously. The fact that her body leaned back a little was suggestive of her reluctance and doubt. Drawing level with him, she looked into Whitman's face, awaiting his answer.

'I'll explain later,' he promised her, adding, 'it'll be a whole heap better than you working back there in the Blue Goose.'

'I suppose so,' she answered logically, as they went down the hill together.

Behind them the Blue Goose piano was thumping. Male and female voices were joined in a not discordant rendition of *'Old Folks at Home'*. With the Prospect Hill coulee acting as a sound trap, the music and singing was as loud as if they were actually back up there in Rosie Diamond's place.

'My name's Ben Whitman,' he told her, anxious to know what she was called. Knowing her name would bring her closer to him.

'Ruby Malone.'

'You almost smiled just then, Ruby,' he teased her.

'If I did, make the most of it. I don't often smile,' she warned him.

He liked her style. Women out here were either chasing money or seeking a husband. Both ambitions made them subservient. Ruby Malone's cool show of independence was refreshing.

They had reached the start of the Main Strip. The lights outside honkytonk saloons were flaring, and the sounds of revelry came from inside. Riders were entering town; some already rowdy in anticipation of a night of fun, while others rode in a brooding silence. Either type could be dangerous. Whitman had learned long ago that it was foolish to generalize when men carried guns on their hips.

He guided her to an hotel. Through the lighted, curtainless window they could see that the dining-room was packed. But there were a few empty tables. The smell of cooked food reached out to them. Aware of it stirring a hunger he hadn't known he had, Whitman recognized what an effect the aroma must be having on her.

Ruby Malone stopped as they went in the hotel door. Turning to him, beautiful face very serious, eyes finding and holding his, she cautioned him, 'You have it wrong if you're expecting me to sing for my supper, Whitman!'

'I've just rescued you from Rosie Diamond,' Whitman answered, 'so why would I be expecting something from you?'

'I suppose that makes sense,' she acknowledged dully, as they stood in the dining-room doorway, looking for the nearest empty table. She went on suspiciously, 'But you must want something from me.'

'All I ask is that you listen to a proposition I want to put to you, Ruby,' he said.

'I'm happy to do that,' she assured him. 'As you said, whatever it is is sure to be preferable to the alternative.'

She was walking on ahead of him then, heading for a table. He said, 'You won't regret this, Ruby.'

From behind her he saw the shrug of Ruby's shoulders and caught the flatly spoken words that she uttered without turning her head. 'What's one more regret when added to a lifetime of them!'

★ ★ ★

'We assumed that the poor girl had found her husband strung up like that, and had just run off,' Pearl Mead said. 'And who could blame her, after all? It must have been an awful shock.'

'We didn't even know she was married. All the time we knowed her we just took it natural-like that she was a widow-woman.' Martin Mead wanted to have as much say as his wife.

Nodding to acknowledge that he had heard what the middle-aged couple had told him, a disappointed Asa Harker took a sip of the coffee they had made for him. On learning that Edward Malone's wife had worked for these people for a number of years, he had been confident when calling at the farm that he was reaching the end of a long and meandering trail. But they knew next to nothing about the woman, and hadn't even known that she had a husband. It was depressing to realize that he had not reached an ending, but yet another beginning.

'She was a lovely woman, so sweet-natured.' Pearl Mead, old before her time, gave him useless information.

'You don't know where she might have gone?' Harker asked. 'Did she ever mention relatives or friends?'

'Never,' Martin Mead was adamant. 'Never gave anything about herself, which I find strange now.'

'What about where she came from, did she ever mention that?' Harker tried.

'No.' Pearl Mead shook her grey head. 'She was a good worker but not given to talking, Mr Harker. When we did speak it was about everyday things.'

There was a sudden commotion outside. Chickens were squawking and pigs screaming. Harker assumed that either the birds or the swine were fighting, which had alarmed the non-combatants. Mead went to take a look out of the window. The noise was subsiding and the farmer, apparently satisfied that all was well, came back to sit down and ask Harker a question.

'Who'd you say you work for, son?'

'I'm an investigator for Wells Fargo,' Harker reiterated, noticing not for the first time how isolated living seemed to destroy or slow down the working of both the mind and the memory.

'And this is a robbery involving a large sum of money?' Pearl Mead asked, in a voice hushed by awe.

'Yes ma'am,' Harker confirmed. 'They hit an office of ours down in Wyoming, and I've followed them through to Montana.'

That was something of an exaggeration. He had trailed a six-man gang up as far as the Yellowstone River. Since then it had been less a case of tracking and more a matter of guessing. The identities of the members of the gang were still unknown to

Harker. In a remarkable lucky break, the sort of thing that rarely came his way, Harker had stayed overnight with a homesteader just after crossing the border into Montana. The sod-buster had been no great shakes in the head department, being limited to moaning about last year's crop and hoping for better things this year. It was the not unattractive wife who had been ready to trade information for Harker taking an interest in her needs. By more or less promising that he would offer a bit more than friendship when her husband gave them the opportunity by going out into the fields, Harker had learned from her that a man named Edward Malone had recently stopped by. Malone, said the homesteader's wife, had been in an agitated state. By snooping when Malone was asleep, presumably after having sampled her special brand of hospitality, she had discovered that he carried a saddle-bag that was jampacked with money.

'And Ruby's husband was one of

the gang?' Mead wrapped a whistle of astonishment round his words.

'Maybe,' Harker replied.

Harker couldn't definitely place Malone anywhere in the robbery. He had no trouble in picking up the other man's trail from the homestead. The problem came from neither the horse's hoofprints nor Malone's footprints matching the gang Harker had followed from Wyoming. His guess was that Malone had been no more than a courier carrying the money for the gang so that they couldn't be linked with it if caught.

'But you don't know who killed Ruby's man?' Pearl Mead enquired.

'Not yet,' Harker replied bitterly. There had been so much traffic to and from the woods where Malone had been found that all tracks for miles around had been obliterated.

'But you surely don't think that Ruby was involved with any of this?' a shocked Mead asked.

'I have no reason to believe so,'

Harker lied, to save the couple from any distress.

In his opinion Edward Malone was lynched because he had not handed over the vast amount of money entrusted to him. Which meant that he must have passed it on. The only person he had been likely to pass it to was his wife. Harker was convinced that Ruby Malone had the money. By finding her he could recover the money, while at the same time use her as the bait to catch the gang.

'Thanks for your help and the coffee, folks,' he said, standing to leave.

'There's more in the pot,' Pearl Mead said invitingly.

'Yes, rest awhile, son,' her husband coaxed. 'You look right tuckered.'

Neither of them wanted him to leave. In their now sexless marriage they had said everything they had to say to each other, probably more than once. They needed a third person, a replacement for Ruby Malone. They were leading harsh, solitary, lives, with nothing but starkly lonely deaths to look forward to.

'Duty calls, I'm afraid,' Harker said, to excuse himself.

Outside, accepting Martin Mead's enthusiastic handshake, he asked, 'Could you tell me what Ruby Malone looks like?'

'She's a lovely woman,' Pearl Mead said. 'Long hair, the colour of corn.'

As he put a foot in the stirrup to pull himself up, Harker heard Mead say, with the kind of reverence reserved for a goddess, 'You'll know her when you see her.'

That was a profound statement to come from a man of the soil, and the words echoed and re-echoed inside of Asa Harker's head as he rode away.

★ ★ ★

Bowbridge was a badly planned, sprawling town which gave the impression of being bigger than it was. Most of the town could be ignored, as all commerce and places of entertainment were contained within an area called The Point. This was a triangular spit of land on the extreme east of Bowbridge, formed by two deep ravines that extended from the river in a giant V, while almost the full length of the third side was taken up by a stockyard.

The First National Bank of Bowbridge stood at the corner of Fourth Avenue and 20th Street. Inside, the building didn't live up to the promise of the front it showed to the street. The banking room was large and oblong in shape. Two-thirds of the way back it was divided by a railing extending from the north wall to the vault. Behind this rail worked two tellers, O.S. Ottley, an ageing man with the edgy fussiness of someone who has been on intimate terms with other people's money for too long, and Josie Simpson, an amiable lad who had yet to come to terms with finding himself working in a bank.

What terrified young Josie most of

all was the door leading to the rear room. In bold letters on that door was the word 'President'. and in the room behind the door was the fearsome G. Joshua Bentley. In the three years that Josie Simpson had been at the bank, Bentley had never spoken to him. The president had shouted many times, but that wasn't the same as talking.

So Josie was filled with trepidation as, out of necessity, he headed for that dreaded door. Fate was unkind to him. No, more than that, it was cruel. It was mid-afternoon. In just over an hour the doors would close to the public and the real counting of the day would begin. Why did this customer have to arrive right now to spoil an otherwise reasonably peaceful day for Josie?

The reply to his knock was more the coughing bark of a prairie dog than it was an invitation to enter. Playing it safe. Josie put just his head and part of his upper body into the room first. His boss, balding, sweating, and with a waxed moustache sticking out like the horns of a Texas steer, was shifting papers about, pointlessly in Josie's opinion, on his desk.

'What is it, Simpson?' G. Joshua Bentley half-shouted. He had little tolerance where ordinary employees were concerned, and none at all in the case of young novices.

'A lady has asked to see you, sir.'

As he felt his anger rise, so did the slashing stomach pain, which was becoming more frequent of late, making it necessary for Bentley to fight an urge to bend over double. Stifling a gasp caused by the agony, he said, 'If it's something you're incapable of dealing with, get Ottley to see the woman!'

Trembling from head to foot, Josie Simpson, abject terror registering on his face, stepped into the room, shut the door behind him and started to do a ludicrous tip-toeing towards the desk.

'What are you up to, boy?' Bentley roared at Simpson's effrontery. 'Have you taken leave of your senses?'

By the desk now, Josie said in a frantic whisper, 'Please, sir. This lady says that she knows of a plot to rob the bank.'

The pain knifed across Bentley's stomach; sweat broke out in large globules across his brow. Then the pain became a dull ache, leaving Bentley alone to stare into the horrible abyss of the greatest fear in his life. In times that became more lawless daily, with gangs of armed robbers using violence to take what didn't belong to them, Bowbridge and its bank had been left in peace to date. Now that was about to end, as he had dreaded. Realizing that he was now every bit as frightened as his shaking young employee, he fought for control so that his voice would at least sound something like normal.

'You had best show the lady in, Simpson.'

Bentley hadn't known what to expect, but he hadn't prepared himself for the golden-haired beauty who stepped in to fill his office with her presence and a fragrance that he wasn't sure was real or imagined. Having married with an eye to promotion rather than anything to do with the flesh, G. Joshua Bentley was not immune to a lovely woman. This one was well-dressed and expensively groomed. It didn't please him to see a man, just as expensively dressed and well turned-out as she, enter the office behind her as he stood.

'I am Mrs Ruth Mellon,' the woman nervously introduced herself. 'I hope you won't mind but I am so frightened by what I have learned, that I have asked my husband to accompany me.'

'Very wise, Mrs Mellon, very wise,' Bentley said, gesturing for her to take the chair opposite to him. It was the only spare chair in the room, but the husband stood behind her without demur as she sat. He even flashed Bentley a friendly smile. He was a handsome fellow indeed. The bank president both hated him and envied him his woman.

'My clerk informed me of the nature

of your visit, madam,' Bentley began, trying not to rush in his eagerness to know what the impending tragedy that he must avert was all about. 'Do you have any idea when this supposed robbery is to be committed?'

'Oh yes,' she nodded gravely, and Bentley wished that she was here for a less harrowing reason, so that he could enjoy looking at her lovely face. 'I have learned that your bank is to be raided this very afternoon.'

Bentley's sweat went cold on him, making his skin feel as if he had been embalmed in ice. This was worse than he thought. The Bowbridge town marshal had crippling arthritis that slowed his every movement, and Sheriff Clinger was out of town.

'Could you tell me from whom you learned of this plot, madam?' he enquired, much steadier of voice than he had expected. The man standing behind the woman cleared his throat to draw Bentley's attention to him.

Grinning at Bentley, the man said,

'I can answer that. She learned it from me.' He reached inside of his jacket to bring out a six-gun and point it at a quaking Bentley. 'Now, if you wouldn't mind signing a cheque for twenty-five thousand dollars, my *wife*, your good self, and me, will go out there, real easy-like, and cash it.'

3

Ella Berry had no illusions about herself. Though her figure was good and she was reasonably pretty, Ella faded into the Blue Goose decor when compared to any of the five voluptuous girls who made up Rosie Diamond's workforce. Ella had come West with the Verdan Concert Entertainers, a family musical troupe. There had been a father, mother, two sons, a daughter and Ella, and the group's first and last performance had been in a Bannon saloon. An irate Elaine Verdan, the mother, had taken the first stage out of town after finding her husband in bed with the busty saloon owner. A half-drunken gunslinger looking for fun had chased the two effeminate sons out of Bannon, and the daughter, bewildered by what had happened to her family, had taken off with a whiskey drummer.

Left without anyone to sing with or talk to, Ella had made her way up Prospect Hill. The Blue Goose had no opening for a singer of the kind of songs Ella had learned to sing. In fact, Rosie Diamond hadn't been prepared to offer her anything until she noticed that Ella had an off-beat attraction for men. When the owner of the Blue Goose made an offer that any decent girl would reject outright, Ella, a decent girl but with no alternative means of survival, accepted.

Ella had taken some time to adapt to a thoroughly unpleasant way of life. What sustained her was the mistake that no girl in her new profession was permitted to make: Ella Berry had fallen in love with a client. This was something that she kept to herself, not even giving him a hint about how she felt. She was pretty sure that he had guessed her feelings for him, and didn't think she was fooling herself by believing that he felt the same way about her.

When he was at the house she was happy. At all other times, Ella felt an aching loneliness, for she had never quite made it with Rosie Diamond and the other girls; she had never fitted in. That was why it came as a surprise when a stranger rode up asking especially for her. Rosie Diamond couldn't fathom it either. The brothel-owner was suspicious at first, but became her usual sweet self when the man made the customary payment in advance.

Young and curly-haired, he would have been ruggedly handsome had not there been a hardness about him, a toughness that made him unapproachable. Poised and courteous, he let Ella know quickly that all he wanted was to talk; to ask questions.

'I understand that you know a man named Ben Whitman very well,' he began, his presence disturbing her, mainly because the gun he wore, slung low and tied to his thigh, was somehow a part of him. It was as if he and the weapon had shared so much together that they couldn't be separated.

This direct approach alarmed Ella. Determined not to harm Ben Whitman in any way, she asked firmly, 'Are you John Law?'

'No,' he shook his head of bronze-coloured curls. 'I'm a detective.'

'A Pinkerton man?' Ella enquired, a little shocked to hear herself asking these questions. A few months ago she wouldn't have used the term 'John Law', and she had known nothing of organizations such as the Pinkerton Agency. Ella was aware that she had changed a lot over the past few months, and it wasn't for the better.

'I work for Wells Fargo,' he explained. 'My name's Asalah Harker, miss.'

'Everyone about here calls me Ella, Mr Harker,' she told him shyly.

For all his inquisitiveness, she liked the man.

'Then I'll do the same, Ella, and you'd better call me Asa, I guess,' he said, smiling for the first time. To

Ella, the smile was a beautiful thing that changed his whole countenance. He was continuing. 'I'm after some men who robbed one of our offices.'

'And you believe Ben is one of them?' she asked, praying that he would deny this. Aware that the man she loved lived on the periphery of the outlaw world, Ella nourished the hope that things might change and the two of them could be together before he committed a serious crime.

'No,' Harker assured her, and she could tell he was puzzled by her interest in Whitman. 'I know that he isn't. But I think that he can help me. It seems he knows a woman I want to talk to. I'm told she came up here the last time Whitman was around.'

A great unhappiness swelled like a balloon inside of Ella. She'd heard talk of the woman who had been loitering outside the Blue Goose when she'd last seen Ben. She enquired miserably, 'Is this that really beautiful woman they've been talking about?'

'I've never seen her, but that's what they say,' Harker replied.

'What has she to do with Ben Whitman?' Ella asked, knowing that she would hate the answer.

'I'm told they may well have left Bannon together,' Harker said, oblivious to the anguish he was causing her. 'Do you know where he might go?'

'He never told me anything about himself,' Ella said quickly, too quickly. Something which Harker didn't miss.

'That's it then,' he told her, plainly disappointed, but still managing one of his special smiles for her. 'You look after yourself, Ella.'

She nodded numbly. Ella was completely devastated by the knowledge that Ben Whitman, the man who carried all her hopes, present and future, had gone off with the golden-haired beauty who had caused such a stir here on Prospect Hill.

'Asa!' she called, when he was by the door. When he turned she asked, 'Can I trust you?'

That was a ridiculous question for a girl to ask a man in a house of ill-fame. Rather, it would have been ridiculous to ask it of any man other than Asa Harker. Instinctively, Ella felt that he was a man on whom she could rely.

'You can trust me, Ella.'

'Ben said that he was heading for Bowbridge.'

Absorbing this information for a moment, Harker said, 'Thank you,' waved a hand at her, and left.

★ ★ ★

'That's mighty fine handwriting, Mr Bentley,' said Whitman in a mocking, complimentary way as he looked at the completed cheque in the bank president's trembling hands. 'All we have to do now is go out there, nice and easy-like, and turn that into cash. Keep in mind though that this Colt will be under my coat; it will be pointing at the middle of your back.'

Taking the large canvas bag Whitman

passed to her, an already thrilled Ruby Malone felt her excitement increase. At the same time she detested herself for being a hypocrite. Having condemned her late husband for his criminal activities, here she was robbing a bank. It didn't help that circumstances had forced her into it, for a woman couldn't live alone in this hard country. She also felt guilty about not often thinking of Edward. Her excuse was that she was trying to remember him as he once was, not as he had been with his face purpled and features grotesquely distorted as he swung from a tree. Ruby doubted that she would ever regain a mental picture of how Edward had looked when she had first known and loved him.

Being in the company of Ben Whitman eased her conscience. Having treated her with absolute respect since they'd met, he was a smooth operator. Had he wanted to ride into Bowbridge at the head of a gang with guns blazing, then Ruby would have gone in the opposite direction. Instead, Whitman used his brains, and was so calm that she had swiftly come to admire him. He was moving them out into the main section of the bank now, single-file, with Bentley in the lead. It came as relief for Ruby that there were no customers present, although she didn't doubt that Whitman had a contingency plan if there had been.

'Close up the bank, Simpson,' the president, having been briefed by Whitman, ordered hoarsely.

While the older teller looked on, suspicion evident on his red face, the lad, bank-trained and disciplined, looked at the yellowing face of the bank clock. The boy protested, mildly but quaveringly, 'There's eight minutes to go yet, sir.'

'Do as I say, boy!' Bentley thundered.

Ruby couldn't help feeling sorry for the bank president, who had perspired so profusely when writing out the cheque that the fetid stench of his sweat had filled the office.

Whitman had timed things well. With

the bank due to close, the locked door would not attract the attention of anyone outside.

Simpson slid the bolts while Bentley placed the cheque on the counter in front of the elderly teller. 'Open the vault, Ottley.'

'But, sir . . . ' Ottley, too devoted an employee to do anything detrimental to the bank, objected.

'Do as I say, Ottley.'

'Sir . . . ' Ottley, fittingly subservient, reached under the counter.

That was where Whitman's plans came suddenly and shatteringly apart. Ruby assumed that, like her, Whitman thought that Ottley was reaching for the key to the vault. They had misjudged the old man, had seriously underrated him.

With his small, fat body struggling, Ottley straightened up with a scattergun clutched in a pair of chubby, inadequate hands. The barrel had been sawn short, but still it was too much for the old and inexperienced cashier to handle.

Whether or not he intended to, Ottley fired the weapon as he swung it up.

There was a terrific explosion that knocked Ottley back against the wall, the shotgun falling from his hands to clatter heavily on the floor. Feeling a stinging in her right forearm, Ruby saw the main part of the shot shatter a window high up in the front wall of the bank. Heavy pieces of the broken glass were falling out into the street. With the town almost certainly alerted, Whitman sprang into action.

Grabbing the elderly teller, he threw him in the direction of the vault, telling him urgently, 'Open it up, old man, and make it quick.'

Fumbling with the key, Ottley, after what seemed an eternity to Ruby, swung open the heavy door. The bank president, apparently resigned to being robbed, had slumped back to rest against his office door. Whitman, taking the bag back from Ruby, glanced at her hand. Taking a look herself, Ruby saw a trickle of blood running down from her sleeve. There was no pain now, no discomfort of any kind.

'It's nothing,' she assured Whitman. 'One or two bits of shot must have caught me.'

Nodding, satisfied that she was all right, Whitman speedily took money from the vault and put it into the bag. Simpson, who had been paralyzed by fear from the noise made by the scattergun and the disintegrating window, suddenly came to life from his position by the door. In a total panic, the boy rushed across the bank in the direction of the vault. Judging the lad's mad charge to be nothing but some kind of reflex action, Ruby, nevertheless, was not prepared to take a chance. Snaking out her right foot she tripped Simpson. The boy crashed headlong into the counter. Dazed, he slid down to sit on the floor and stayed there.

With his bag full, Whitman used his gun to herd Bentley and Ottley into the president's office. Grabbing Simpson's collar, he pulled the boy, who was awake but lifeless, across the floor to toss him into the office, too. Reaching, Whitman retrieved the key, shut the door and locked it from the outside.

They went out through the front door fast and together, not knowing what to expect. At the hitching post directly outside, Whitman's roan waited beside the Indian pony he had bought for Ruby. The town was quiet.

As they untied the reins, she speculated to Whitman, 'It doesn't look as if anyone heard the shot and the breaking of the window.'

'Don't be too sure,' Whitman warned as they mounted up. 'We have to ride down through that street, and they could be waiting for us.'

They were pulling on the reins, ready to move off, when a youth sprang up from where he had been crouching beside a hardware store.

He ran across the street shouting, 'Robbery! Robbery! They've just come out the bank!'

As Ruby and Whitman sent their horses at a gallop down the street, three men alerted by the youth's shout, all carrying rifles, all wearing the silver badges of lawmen, appeared on the board sidewalk to the right of Ruby and Whitman.

The danger increased the excitement Ruby had felt since entering the bank. With the pony stretched to its limit beneath her, it was exhilarating to feel the wind against her face. For the first time ever she felt really alive. The young man was running away from them down the street on her left, still yelling the alarm. Swinging her horse over, Ruby rode in close to the buildings, so tight that a man coming out through a doorway to see what was causing the commotion, was caught by the shoulder of her horse and sent crashing back inside.

Closing in on the youth, held completely in the thrill of the chase, Ruby freed her left foot from the stirrup. Bending her knee, keeping her booted foot sole thrust out in front of her, she caught the youth hard in the centre of his back.

Propelled forward with such force that his feet were lifted from the ground, the young man hit the horizontal rail of a hitching rack, waist high. As Ruby pulled her horse back to the centre of the street to ride beside Whitman, she saw the youth spinning over and over on the rail like an accomplished acrobat.

Then bullets were whistling close to them as they rode. The three men, a sheriff and his deputies or whatever, had all dropped to one knee and were firing rifles. Ruby knew that it could only be a matter of seconds before one, or probably both of them were hit. But Whitman had drawn his six-shooter. Firing with incredible accuracy from the saddle of a galloping horse, he cut the danger by a third. As Whitman's bullets smashed the windows of the building behind him, one of the riflemen dropped face down on the boardwalk to avoid being hit.

Seeing this, Ruby drew her Henry rifle from its scabbard. Looping the reins of her horse round the saddle horn, she gripped with her knees as she turned, rifle to her shoulder, to fire at the remaining two men.

Glass shards flew about in the air, and huge splinters of wood were ripped from the building behind the men. It was too much for them. All three crawled in through the door behind them.

Replacing her rifle and retrieving her reins, Ruby brought her horse in close to Whitman as they reached the end of the street to head out of town.

'Where did you learn to ride and shoot like that?' an astonished Whitman shouted to her.

'Like what?' she yelled back, being deliberately obtuse so as to retain her modesty.

This made Ben Whitman laugh. With his stetson blown back, held on only by the cord around his neck, he had a handsome wildness to him that wasn't lost on Ruby. As they allowed their horses to slow, he patted the bag that was crammed full of money, telling her with a grin, 'Seeing as you helped out a bit back there, Ruby, I might consider giving you a share of this.'

'If you don't,' she cautioned him, leaning forward a little in the saddle to caress the stock of the Henry rifle, 'I'll show you what I can really do with this.'

She heard Whitman chuckle as she waited for some kind of anti-climax to hit her. Although she had never experienced anything like this, she knew that life invariably knocked you back after giving you a lift. But Ruby at last accepted that it wouldn't happen. Instead she was filled with elation and she reached up and unfastened her hair. As it fell, she shook her head from side to side to help it settle. Then, suddenly spurring her horse, she let out a wild yell without having any idea where it came from. As abandoned as a Sioux brave, she galloped off.

Spurring his horse, Whitman caught up with her. They rode together, laughing wildly, both as free as the wind that lifted her long golden hair, streaming out behind her.

★ ★ ★

Ruby Malone further intrigued Asa Harker when he found that Bannon, a town with a transient population, remembered her. The hotel proprietor, an Englishman with impeccable manners and an apparent susceptibility to strikingly beautiful women, recalled that she had dined in his restaurant with a 'young gentleman', whom Harker took to be Ben Whitman. Both 'this lady with truly remarkable looks', and the 'young gentleman', had stayed for that one night in the hotel.

'They shared a room,' Harker stated rather than asked.

This shocked the Englishman. 'My dear fellow, they most certainly didn't.

My gracious, no. She wasn't that kind of lady at all. The young gentlemen did pay for both rooms, but I assure you that it was all very correct and proper. Am I right in thinking that you require a room this night, sir?'

'No,' Harker shook his head. He had other enquiries to make elsewhere, then he wanted to be on his way to Bowbridge. He would ride through the night so as not to let their trail cool.

Coming down the steps from the hotel into the street, Harker stood for a moment. Darkness had transformed the town. Sleepy and half-deserted during the day, it was now fully awake. Men and women, all of them pleasure-seekers, passed by in droves. The three saloons on the main strip were doing good business, if noise was anything to go by.

Rolling a cigarette and lighting it, Harker strolled across the street and entered the nearest saloon. It was so crowded that he needed to shoulder his way to the bar to order a whiskey.

As he drank, weighing up everything around him, a man with a star on his chest and a rifle held in both hands, came in to stand behind the door and look around. A tall, gaunt man with a great hook of an eagle-beak nose, he was plainly the town marshal making his rounds.

'What's the marshal's name?' Harker enquired of an overworked barkeep, who at first resented being asked questions, but then answered sullenly.

'Henry Keswick.'

With a nod of thanks, Harker made his way out of the saloon. Keswick had already left, and he was not out in the street as Harker made his way to a busy restaurant. There he ate a meal to sustain him through the long night ride ahead. Next he went back out into the street to seek and find the town marshal's office.

Stepping into an office that was unoccupied, Harker looked around. There was a battered desk and a rifle rack in which the weapons were secured by a locked chain. Behind the desk was a door leading to cells at the back.

'Henry Keswick?' Harker called.

A voice came from somewhere out back. 'Who's calling my name?'

'I'm Asa Harker,' Harker shouted. 'You don't know me.'

'Darn blast it, Harker, nor do I want to know you. On your way.'

'I have to speak to you, Keswick.' Harker stood his ground.

There was a silence of considerable duration, then Keswick asked, 'If you're carrying a rifle, Harker, let me hear you lay it down on the desk behind you.'

'I don't have a rifle.'

'You toting a six-gun, Harker?'

'I am,' Harker replied.

'Well, unbuckle your belt, and let me hear that drop on the table,' Keswick instructed.

Obeying, Harker let his gunbelt fall with a thud. Then the marshal came out from the back, holding a rifle trained on Harker, who remarked, 'You're careful, Keswick.'

'I'm alive, Harker,' was the marshal's rejoinder.

'Is Bannon that bad?' Harker enquired.

'Worse,' Keswick replied glumly. 'Now, what are you here to hassle me about, Harker?'

Explaining that he was with Wells Fargo and showing his papers, Harker asked, 'What do you know of a man named Ben Whitman?'

'Never heard of him,' Keswick replied emphatically. 'I could check the name with Sheriff Wilson in the morning.'

'I'm leaving town now,' Harker explained.

'That's too bad,' Keswick said, then looked hopefully at Harker. 'I was making coffee when you turned up, Harker. Will you join me?'

Accepting the offer, Harker sat in an empty cell with Keswick, getting to like the big-nosed man as he listened to the trials and tribulations of being marshal in a town like Bannon. They shared Harker's makings and then he left.

Harker made his way to the livery stables in River Street at the bottom of town to collect his horse. The hostler there had met Ben Whitman. He remembered because he had sold Whitman an Indian pony. That had been useful information for Harker. It told him that Ruby Malone was not on foot.

There was no one at the stables when he saddled his horse and headed out of town. He rode into a moonless night, the lack of light increasing his habitual caution. Catching movement up ahead where a collection of boulders and some dead trees provided cover for a man and a horse, Harker reined in and dismounted.

Going off at a tangent on foot, he came in at the rear of the boulders to see a mounted figure facing the trail, plainly waiting for him to come along.

The rider gave a little jump as he ordered, 'Whoever you are, raise your hands above your head. Keep them on show while you get down off that horse.'

'It's me, Asa,' a girl's voice answered. 'It's Ella. I want to ride with you to find Ben.'

4

Ben Whitman's stunning companion had got him noticed. His and Ruby's descriptions had been circulated to sheriffs' offices beyond the territory in which they operated. Previously a nonentity in a land teeming with outlaws, he had now achieved something like a star billing. It was the novelty factor of his crimes, not the enormity of them, that had brought him a modest fame that he thoroughly enjoyed. It didn't worry him that he shared the notoriety with Ruby. The part she played appealed to the imagination of the newspapers and the public in general. More print had been used to describe her beauty than was allotted to the amount of money they had stolen. No reward had yet been offered, but he accepted that it was just a matter of time before a price would be put on their heads. That would be something of an accolade for him, but he didn't know how Ruby would take it. She was aloof except for the times when the chips were down, when danger threatened.

In the wake of the successful Bowbridge robbery, they had pulled a similar stunt at a bank in Demsville. Posing as customers wanting to open an account, they had encouraged the greed of the partners operating the bank, Oliver Nimrod and George W. Cousins. Ruby, elegantly dressed and coiffured, had passed Nimrod a hundred-dollar bill to open an account.

A fawning Nimrod had taken the bill, his smile replaced by a frown as he studied it. Excusing himself, Nimrod had gone over to his partner, and the two of them engaged in an animated, low-voiced discussion. Nimrod had come back to them, with Cousins close on his heels.

'I am so sorry, madam,' Nimrod apologized, 'but this bill is counterfeit.'

Whitman had taken the dollar bill to glance at it briefly before saying, 'I reckon it is.' Tucking the bill inside his jacket he quickly pulled out a business-like Colt. With a smile he said, 'But this is real, Mr Nimrod. Open the vault.'

Quickly, Ruby retrieved her faithful Henry rifle ftom her horse and took up a position inside the open door. Neither Nimrod nor Cousins were made of heroic stuff. Obediently they crammed money into the wheat sack Whitman had passed them. A problem occurred when a man stepped unwittingly into the bank. From the corner of his eye, Whitman saw it was a heavily built farmer who was standing, staring in shock at the robbery in progress.

Unable to understand why Ruby had not warned him of the newcomer, Whitman grinned to himself as she proved he had been a fool to doubt her.

Having pulled herself tight in behind the door, Ruby jabbed her Henry rifle forward, stock first, to catch the farmer a heavy blow in the back that sent him reeling. Taking a step forward, she swung the Henry again to catch him a glancing blow on the jaw that was enough to fell him. Dropping to the floor, the farmer sat up, propping his back against a wall as he looked at Ruby in astonishment and fear.

With the barrel of the rifle now pointing at the farmer, Ruby told him, 'You as much as break wind and I'll drill you.'

They had got away then, leaving town without hindrance and with close to $33,000 in the sack.

After that, guessing that every bank over a wide area would be prepared for them and their unusual methods, they changed targets. Two days later they were lurking in the brush beside a road along which a Wells Fargo coach was lumbering through the dust toward them.

Timing it right, they stepped out in front of the stage, the driver hauling the coach to a halt. With Ruby and her Henry covering the driver and guard up on the box, Whitman, his .45 in his hand, opened the door and ordered the seven passengers to line up in the road. There were four men of varying ages and style, and three women. Of the latter, two were matronly while the third was young and pretty.

Starting with the men, Whitman ordered the passengers to produce their valuables. He enjoyed the indignation of men who could well afford to lose a few of their personal possessions, and couldn't resist flirting with the girl passenger so that she blushed prettily.

Ruby became daring. When everyone was back in the coach, she rode up close to perform the act that was becoming her trademark. Letting her hair fall, she shook her head vigorously to let it flow loosely, then she and Whitman galloped away.

It wasn't so lucrative as robbing banks, but they came away with an impressive amount of jewellery, $130 collected from the passengers, and the Wells Fargo express package containing $850.

With a need to stay out of sight for a while, and with word of their exploits preceding them, they received a tentative welcome in Lolo Valley. Here they joined, but were not fully accepted into, a community of desperadoes. It was an army made up of killers, rustlers, robbers, horsethieves and fugitives, into which was mixed a number of dance-hall girls. They all resided in smoky cabins, with a large saloon supplying whiskey and entertainment. Every law officer in the land was aware that this grubby city of sin existed, but a force of at least 200 men would be needed to do anything about Lolo Valley.

A tacit rule that everyone in the valley obeyed was that there would be no lawlessness in the immediate area. When provisions were needed from the farms close to Lolo Valley, or beef needed from a local rancher, each and every item was paid for, and the farmers and ranchers treated with respect. This was one of the principal reasons why the outlaw community survived and would continue to do so.

It was Emlyn Rodgers, the owner of the saloon, a slim, mild-mannered man of womanish appearance, who offered Whitman and Ruby temporary accommodation.

'There's a room out back you are both welcome to,' he offered, making it sound like generosity, but they guessed there would be some price to pay. Lolo Valley wasn't a place where people were nice to each other.

Rodgers looked quizzically at Ruby when she dumped her Henry rifle noisily on the bar and said firmly, 'Two rooms.'

'That ain't showing much gratitude to Mr Rodgers, Ruby,' a deeply disappointed Whitman complained.

'You are my partner on the road, Whitman, not in the hay,' she told him tersely.

So Ruby was fixed up with a room of

her own, and now, on their first evening there, she sat at a table in the saloon drinking with Whitman. The other women there excused her presence but did not overshadow it. There were four insipid-looking dance-hall girls loitering around wearing vacant smiles, while a woman of sorts stood at the bar with a small group of men. Dressed all in buckskin, the woman, whom they heard referred to as Kate, was big, with her hair pulled back from an ugly face and tied in a bun. With four barmen constantly busy, Rodgers sat on a high stool at one end of the bar, his smooth face wearing the snooty expression of a prima donna as he surveyed his domain. Not far from him, wearing crossed gunbelts and a .44 on each hip, was Claude Viddel, the swarthy, dangerous-looking houseman who was plainly Rodgers' trouble-shooter. An inexpert pianist coaxed a popular tune from the instrument, but it was almost unrecognizable due to him missing every fourth or fifth beat.

Ruby looked sleepy to Whitman, but he had learned to take nothing for granted where she was concerned. His way of life had confined his relationships to females with shallow personalities. Ruby Malone was so deep that she was fascinating, but in addition was more than a little frightening. Not that she scared him in a physical way; it was something very different to that.

'Well, Ruby, where do we go from here?' Whitman asked, when the silence between them became uncomfortable, as it so often did.

'*We*?' she enquired, increasing his feeling of insecurity where she was concerned.

'I thought we made a good team,' he replied defensively.

'Likely we do,' she conceded with a nod, 'but I've got something that I have to do.'

'Whatever it is, it won't bring in the sort of money you and me can make together, Ruby,' Whitman warned her.

'If I'm not mistaken,' she told him

thoughtfully, 'it would take us twenty years to steal the sort of money involved in what I'm talking about.'

Leaning toward her, an avid Whitman said, 'I'm interested, tell me?'

Indecision made Ruby remain silent. She looked around her as if seeking guidance from the disorderly scene in the saloon. There was some kind of argument going on between the buckskin-clad woman and two of the men she was with.

'I suppose I could use your help, and you'd be well rewarded,' she said, so quietly that he had to move closer to catch her words. 'But before I tell you, I want your solemn promise that, should you not want to go along with me, you will not breathe a word of what I say to anyone.'

'I'm an honourable man.' He looked at her wide-eyed.

'I don't think those bank managers and the folk on the stagecoach would agree with that,' Ruby said wryly.

He grinned at her. 'They were just

people. You're special, Ruby. You can rely on me.'

Whitman was a robber and a trickster, but Ruby was certain he would never let her down. Slowly, she began the tale of her disjointed, unhappy married life, coming through to Edward's final visit, the money-packed saddle-bag, and the sheriff's posse that had turned into a lynch party.

'Turps Hallam!' Whitman mused, when she had finished speaking. Remembrance brightened his face. 'Sure, I know of him. He's a sheriff down near Yellowstone River. He hangs out in a bitch of a town called Tascosa.'

There was uproar then as the woman in buckskin picked up a bottle by the neck, the liquor inside bubbling out. Smashing the bottle on the edge of the counter, she pushed the jagged edges into the face of one of the men she had been arguing with. He staggered back, clutching his face with both hands, blood running out between his fingers. The second man drew a bowie knife as the woman turned to him, the bottle with its sharp, blood-dripping edges held menacingly.

Claude Viddel moved so fast that neither Whitman nor Ruby saw how he got to the trouble spot. Stepping past the man with the knife, Viddel lashed out with his right foot to kick the woman in the stomach who grunted wheezily as the breath was knocked out of her. But the woman was tough. Staying upright, the pain from the kick evident on her face, she swung her bottle at the houseman. Threading his left arm under hers, entwining it, Viddel applied pressure. There came three consecutive sounds, a dull sucking noise as the buckskin-clad woman's arm was wrenched from its socket, a mighty crack as the bone in her upper arm snapped, and a piercing howl of agony that came ripping out of her wide-open mouth.

Whitman tensed, ready to go to

the houseman's aid as the man with the knife lunged, aiming at Viddel's back. Reaching out to grab Whitman's shoulder to hold him back, Ruby needn't have bothered. Viddel required no help. Without turning, the houseman was somehow aware of everything going on behind him. Viddel drove the elbow of his right arm back into the other man's face, smashing his mouth in with such force that the lower part of the knifeman's face seemed to be driven right back into his neck. Pivoting on one heel, the houseman came round to grab the wrist of the knife hand and pull as again he raised his elbow. This time he crushed the upper part of the face.

Threshing about in agony, the woman lay face down across a table, while the man with the shattered face had fallen to the floor. An awed Whitman whispered, 'I reckon as how he's dead!'

'Be better for him if he is,' Ruby said, a little shaky from the speed and degree of violence she had just witnessed. 'It won't be any fun living without a face.'

Wrapping a whistle of disbelief around his words, Whitman exclaimed, 'I sure wouldn't want to come up against Claude Viddel.'

'I want to get out of this place,' Ruby said fervently. Lolo would serve them as a temporary place of sanctuary, but neither was desperate enough to stay there long term. 'Will it be worth going after this Hallam? It's likely he'll have spent the money by now.'

'No!' Whitman shook his head. 'He must have been part of whatever that robbery was, Ruby, probably the leader. So he'll have to make it look good as sheriff until he's had time to sort things out. Hallam won't be able to make a sudden show of wealth. He'll have stashed the money, and we just got to go on down there and relieve him of it.'

Which will be some kind of justice for Edward, she was thinking humbly when she saw Rodgers heading in their direction. For all his soft looks she could tell that he was a highly dangerous man.

Smiling at them both, he apologized. 'Sorry about that little fracas. We get that sort of thing from time to time. Oh, by the way, you can start earning your keep tomorrow, Ben. Claude's going down to the Fieldings' farm to collect the produce. You can go along with him. We hear there could be a Pinkerton operative down there making out like he's a farmhand.'

'I'll be happy to go along,' Whitman forced himself to say, but when the saloon owner had left them, both he and Ruby had a bad feeling about Lolo Valley.

★ ★ ★

'You understand that this don't alter things between Ben and me,' Ella Berry said morosely, as she folded the blanket that had covered Harker and herself all night.

Smiling inwardly, Harker watched the dust she was making dance about in the weak beams of light a dawn sun was feeding through the holes in the barn. The girl had either forgotten that she had for some time been a whore, or had forced the unpleasant fact from her mind. His amusement ended as soon as he realized how cruel it was. Ella was a sweet girl who had proved she was able to adapt fluidly to each situation as it arose.

'If me and Ben should ever meet, then I won't tell him,' Harker promised, shaking his clothes free of insects before getting into them.

Both Ella and he had used farm clothing as a disguise. Having satisfied himself that Ruby Malone and Ben Whitman were holed up in Lolo Valley, this farm was the closest Harker could get to the outlaw community. They had posed as a man and wife, drifters seeking farm work. Jud Fielding had taken them on, throwing in the opportunity to bed down in straw in the barn to balance out the poor pay that he offered.

Yet to formulate a plan, and keenly aware that riding into Lolo Valley was out of the question, Harker had used a night with the willing Ella as a diversion. Right now, in the cold light of dawn, he was regretting it just as much as she apparently was.

Harker went outside, stretching as he filled his lungs with air so fresh that it caused a slight, far from unpleasant pain inside his chest. Luck had been with him so far. Whitman and the woman should have stuck to robbing banks. Hitting the Wells Fargo stage had been the beginning of what he was determined to make their end. Whitman's horse and Ruby Malone's pony had left what were the only tracks around the hold up. It had been said of Harker that he 'could follow a woodtick on a solid rock', and he'd had no trouble tracking the pair to the outlaw hideout. Ella, bored with the trailing process, had been a liability then, but later she had been invaluable by giving credence to his claim of being an itinerant farmworker.

Not looking forward to a day of hoeing or picking, Harker had to remind himself that the robbing of the stage was not the main crime. It was nothing to the vast amount of money he intended to recover through Ruby Malone. The Wyoming robbery represented the largest single theft ever from Wells Fargo, and he had sworn to retrieve the money and either apprehend or kill those responsible.

Washing in a barrel of rainwater, he was drying himself on a piece of sacking when Nan Fielding walked up to him. Thin and plain-looking, Nan ran the farm with her father. Sensing that she had taken an intense interest in him, Harker was disturbed by it, and he wanted no complications. Nan was looking toward the door of the barn where Ella stood buttoning her shirt.

'I sure hope you and your *wife* had a good night,' Nan said with heavy sarcasm. She raised her voice to Ella. 'Pa wants you up in that field yonder, girl, baggin' up potatoes for a customer that's due this morning.'

When Ella used a little duck of her head to acknowledge she had heard, but remained stationary, Nan shouted angrily at her, 'Well, shake a hoof, girl. We don't pay you to stand around.'

Ella walked off sulkily in the direction Nan had indicated, and the farmer's daughter turned to Harker. 'You work down by the house, Harker. There's a whole heap of sacks of buckwheat want loading on a wagon.'

When Harker got to work it worried him that Jud Fielding wasn't around. But Nan didn't come out of the house until at least an hour had gone by. It had been an hour of hard toil for Harker. who was sweating, while his back ached from work he was not accustomed to.

'I'm cooking succotash for dinner,' she informed him, standing too close to him.

Taking a sideways step to put some distance between them, Harker needn't have bothered. Losing interest in him, she raised a hand to shield her eyes as a wagon with two men on the seat came slowly over the hill. Stopping work to look, Harker saw one man alight and head toward them, while the remaining man moved the wagon over to where Ella was bent at her work.

'This here fella's name's Claude Viddel from up in Lolo Valley,' Nan tersely told Harker. 'He's mean, Harker, real mean.'

With that she went hurriedly into the house. Harker stood facing the swarthy man who was advancing on him. Everything about Viddel, including the two guns that he wore, said he was trouble. He gave Harker a grin as he came up to him.

'Well, now if that don't beat all, a new face about here's as scarce as hen's teeth,' Viddel said. 'Where did you spring up from, sodbuster?'

Harker was saved from answering by

Nan coming out of the house. He noticed that she had tidied her hair and dress for Viddel's sake. This wasn't missed by Viddel, who meaningfully stared her up and down as he took a roll of dollar bills from his pocket. 'The boy with the wagon's picking up the potatoes, Miss Fielding. Here's the greenbacks for your daddy.'

Taking the money, Nan went back into the house while Viddel openly studied Harker, laconically advising him, 'You should do a bit of sparking there, pard. Old Nan's just about ready to thrash around like a short-tailed bull at fly-time.'

Without warning, Viddel flicked out a hand to lift the long flap of the farm shirt that Harker was wearing.

'That's a damn fine gun for a farmhand to be carrying round,' Viddel remarked suspiciously.

Harker shrugged. 'I'm just here to find work.'

'You got a job already,' Viddel said savagely, 'with the goddamned law.'

Turning on his heel, Viddel was walking away as if in disgust. But Harker knew that it wasn't over between him and the Lolo Valley man. In fact, it hadn't yet begun. Unbuttoning his shirt, pulling away the flap from his six-shooter, Harker glanced up to the near horizon formed by the hill. The other man from Lolo Valley had loaded his wagon and was riding away from Ella.

Suddenly turning, Viddel drew both of his guns as he came round. It happened at great speed and, as Harker drew, he doubted that he had shaded the other man. All three guns barked, but Harker's single bullet went home first. It drove into the left breast of Claude Viddel, instantly stopping his heart.

Feeling a bullet pluck at the right sleeve of his shirt, Harker watched Viddel fall while a deafening shrieking started up to his left. Looking round, he first saw a shock-faced Nan Fielding coming to the door of the house, then he saw what was causing all the noise. Viddel's shot had hit a half-grown pig in the head. It hadn't killed the animal, which was rushing around in agony, smashing its bleeding head against anything it came up against, in an attempt to free itself from the intolerable pain it was suffering.

Nan came out to look down at the body of Viddel and shudder. The man on the wagon was getting it away as fast as he could. Ella came running down the hill, while the injured pig continued to scream. It was losing its balance now as it dashed about. Running straight at the wall of the house, the animal hit it head on with such force that it was thrown into a backward somersault. Lying with its pink-legged trotters threshing at the air, its mouth was wide open as it shattered the air with scream after scream.

'You beat Claude Viddel to the draw!' a dazed Nan said, then she raised her voice to Harker. 'The pig!'

Drawing his gun again, just as the

pig regained its feet to begin another crazy run around, Harker fired, putting it out of its misery.

Beckoning Ella to join him as fast as she could, Harker shouted, 'Come on, Ella. We've got to get out of here.'

'It's all right, Asa,' she called to him, breathless from running but elated by something else. 'That was Ben, Ben Whitman, with the wagon. I told him everything and he said that he'll help us.'

'Did you tell him what I am?' Harker groaned, knowing what her answer would be.

'Yes,' she nodded, still gasping for breath. 'At first I couldn't think of the name, but then I remembered. I told him that you were with Wells Fargo. He's promised to come down here after dark.'

Expecting praise, Ella Berry couldn't understand why Harker gave her such a harsh look. He looked down at Viddel and then turned to Nan to ask, 'Will your father be home soon to take care of him?'

Still shaken by what had happened, the farmer's daughter nodded glumly. Taking Ella by the arm, Harker told her, 'We've got to get moving.'

'But . . . what about Ben?' she objected.

Not answering, Harker went to get their horses. Once Whitman told them in the valley that Viddel was dead, then both he and Ella would also be dead if they waited around here. They would have to move out to find a safe place in the hills to watch for Whitman and Ruby Malone. Though Harker knew that the pair would be leaving Lolo Valley without delay, he needed to find out which way they would be heading.

5

'Will we be safe here?' Ruby Malone asked, as she and Whitman rode into Bannon.

It was early evening and the town was quiet. Only three children playing with a cart, and a couple of scavenging dogs afforded them a second glance. Ruby had been on edge since their rushed departure from Lolo Valley. Even Whitman, who was young enough and wild enough to be ignorant of the dangers in life, had admitted that this Wells Fargo man must be really something to have outdrawn Claude Viddel. Initially, most of the population of the valley refused to believe that anyone could have gunned down Viddel in a fair fight. Emlyn Rodgers had been hardest hit by the death of his right-hand man.

'Sure,' Whitman answered her.

'Bannon's so sleepy that the folk here wouldn't look round if you came in firing that Henry rifle of yours.'

Ruby noticed, however, that Whitman made sure that they kept in the shadows cast by buildings as they rode up Main Strip. This increased her nervousness so that she checked with him. 'We won't be staying overnight, will we, Ben?'

'We don't have a choice,' he replied, chilling her because she wanted to be out of this town. 'We need victuals, and none of the stores will open again until morning. What do you say to a good cooked meal, a room, a bath, and a comfortable bed, Ruby?'

All that he said appealed to her, greatly, but such a plan seemed to be full of peril. But she could tell that he wouldn't be deterred. They left their mounts at the livery stables in River Street, but she took her rifle. Although she felt conspicuous on the street carrying the Henry, she desperately needed the reassurance of having it with her.

They went to the same dining-room of the same hotel as before. Ruby welcomed the meal, but was certain that their presence was arousing suspicion. She put her fears in a low voice to Whitman. 'I feel sure that hotel man is watching us!'

Taking a cautious look around, Whitman said, 'You're imagining things. I'll get us a bottle of red-eye each to take up to our rooms. That'll relax you.'

'Just get one,' Ruby said, and he looked at her sharply, searching for the meaning behind what she had said. Because she didn't know what she meant, Ruby kept her eyes averted.

With the meal over they walked together to the desk. Holding the rifle close to her side as she walked, Ruby slid it down to the floor, propped it against the desk as the clerk spun the register on the polished mahogany for them to sign.

Her mind in a turmoil, fear getting the better of her, Ruby spoke as

Whitman picked up the pen. 'I couldn't bear to be alone this night, Ben. Book a room for us together.'

Ruby found the boyish delight on his face to be conversely sweet and off-putting at the same time. There was a constant movement inside of her head so that though she heard the words of Whitman and the clerk as arrangements were made for a room, she couldn't decipher them. Never before had she felt like this, and she couldn't be sure if the cause was a growing attachment to Ben Whitman, the thrill of her new way of life, or the icy dread she had felt since reaching the outskirts of Bannon. She was certainly very different right then than she had been when, with the red-hot tip of a knife, she had dug into her own arm to get out the tiny balls of shot from Ottley, the bank cashier's, scattergun.

As he wrote with one hand and slid the other arm round her waist, at first she kept her body stiff, but she was badly in need of human warmth and companionship. Letting the tension flow out of her body she cuddled against him. When the clerk turned away to get their key, Whitman held her in a one-armed embrace and buried his face in her hair.

'Don't turn around,' a low, harsh voice said from close behind them.

Whitman's arm dropped away from around her waist, Ruby felt her knees give so that she was certain she would fall to the floor. But then a rigidity hit her, stiffening her body from her ankles to her neck. She sensed that Whitman was turning his head, and heard the sharp command repeated behind them.

'Don't turn around! You, ma'am, just nudge that rifle of yours with your knee so that it falls.'

Doing as she was told, Ruby heard her beloved Henry clatter to the floor. Then the man behind was in close. She could tell that the muzzle of a rifle was pressed into Whitman's back while a hand slid between them to unbuckle his gunbelt and pull it off.

'You can turn around now.'

They did so, slowly. Frightened for some reason to look at first, Ruby then raised her eyes. Facing them, a rifle held at his hip and Whitman's gunbelt draped over his shoulder, was a man wearing the badge of town marshal. There was something odd about him that Ruby couldn't place. But when he gestured for them to move a little to one side and, while keeping them covered, bent to pick up her rifle, she saw that he had an extremely large nose.

* * *

Asa Harker walked to the cells with the town marshal. There had been immense relief for Harker when arriving in Bannon, three weeks later than he had intended, to discover that Ben Whitman and Ruby Malone were being held in custody awaiting trial. The delay had been caused by a fever that had struck Ella just hours after they had left Jud Fielding's farm. Harker had nursed her up in the hills, with Ella delirious for long periods. To get by he'd had to trust Jud and Nan Fielding, and even the farmer's strange-minded daughter had helped them by readily providing food. Harker had to sneak down to the farm at night. Emlyn Rodgers had learned his name and had sent out gunmen from the valley with orders to avenge Claude Viddel. Even with food and a supply of water from a nearby stream, Harker had been helpless without medicine. At times he had feared losing Ella.

But she had recovered sufficiently to make the ride to Bannon, although it had weakened her to the extent that he had put her to bed immediately on arrival at the hotel.

'It's out of my hands now,' Keswick was saying. 'Sheriff Wilson took over after I brought them in. The trial begins tomorrow, providing Judge Bower gets here in time.'

This didn't allow Harker much time to find out what he could from Ruby Malone. If she refused to tell him anything, which was a distinct possibility, he wouldn't get another chance if she and Whitman were sent to prison for the robberies they had committed.

'I guess that both of them will be convicted,' Harker said, to test what sort of case there was against them.

With a shake of his head, the marshal voiced his doubts. 'Well, Harker, the evidence against that pair is pretty damn convincing, and Prosecutor Williams ain't never lost a case to my knowledge, but this Ben Whitman's got me sorely puzzled. He must have friends in high places, because Colonel C. T. Alexander has arrived in town to defend both Whitman and the woman.'

Harker had met the colonel many times in different courtrooms, and admired the man if not his principles as a lawyer. A former Confederate officer, Alexander had an old-fashioned southern chivalry that had survived the Civil War which had brought him to prominence. Colonel Alexander now fought his battles in the courtroom, taking the side of the underdog to gain a series of resounding successes. Until he had met and heard what Ruby Malone had to say, Harker couldn't be sure whether the presence of Alexander and a possible acquittal for the woman, was a good or a bad thing for him.

Then he was being ushered into a cell by Henry Keswick, who stayed outside, locking the door before walking away. Harker was left momentarily speechless by the beauty of the golden-haired woman who stood up from a cot to look at him questioningly.

Recovering, he introduced himself. 'I'm Asalah Harker, ma'am, an investigator for Wells Fargo.'

Accepting this with a nod, she took a little while to answer. Harker sensed that she was as affected as he by a powerful, involuntary rapport between them. This was something that he hadn't previously encountered, and he was at a loss to know how to deal with it.

'I don't need to tell you who I am,' she said drily, 'but rather than waste your time I'll say that you won't get whatever it is you want from me.'

'I know what happened to your husband, ma'am,' Harker said. 'I was following him and the gang he was running with. I'm after a bag he was carrying on the night he died.'

'You're after what was in the bag, Harker,' she corrected him with a wry smile, 'and you think that I have it. Believe me, I wouldn't be in here, I wouldn't have become an outlaw, if I had that money.'

Ruby Malone was intelligent as well as lovely, instantly grasping his reason for being there. She was cool, too, not the type that he could use his experience as a detective to trick or trap.

'I accept that you don't have it,'

he said. 'That means whoever it was killed your husband took the bag of money. What can you tell me about them, ma'am?'

Looking him steadily in the eye, having a profound effect on him, she answered, 'It isn't what I *can* tell you, Harker, it's more a matter of what I *choose* to tell you. I don't see you as a man interested in personal gain, so what has made you come all this way after money belonging to someone else?'

'I have a duty to the people to whom the money belongs,' Harker said.

Turning away from him, picking up a short jacket and draping it over her shoulders as if she suddenly felt cold, she spoke quietly, 'I also have a duty to someone.'

Assuming that she was referring to Ben Whitman, Harker accepted that there was no point in trying to seduce her from her loyalty to her partner in the robberies that had been committed. A strong woman, Ruby Malone was not the type to betray anyone. It occurred to him then what was happening. She knew who the men were who had lynched her husband and taken the money, and had enlisted Whitman's help in retrieving the money, and perhaps getting even with the gang. All he needed to do was wait and follow them, either when they were acquitted at the trial or at the end of any prison sentences they might receive.

'Keswick!' he called to the marshal, and to Ruby Malone he said, 'Thank you for your time, ma'am.'

When Keswick unlocked the door to let him out, she called his name. 'Harker.'

'Yes?'

Biting on her lower lip for a moment, she told him, 'If it means anything, I'm sorry.'

Giving her a curt nod, he walked off with Keswick, who asked. 'Did you get anything, Harker?'

'I've made a start,' Harker replied,

'but it might take a mighty long time to reach the end.'

'You strike me as a man with patience,' Keswick said with a hard-faced grin.

'I'm sure going to need to be,' Harker muttered, as he went out of the marshal's office into the street.

Consoling himself that he only had to wait until tomorrow for the trial to decide his next move for him, Harker, who had an odd sense of having brought something of Ruby Malone with him, went back to the hotel. The proprietor hurried toward him, a worried expression on his face.

'Mary is up in your room. That little girl of yours is mighty sick.'

Hurrying up the stairs, Harker found Ella lying on the bed. Mary, a worker in the hotel, was wiping a cold cloth over her face, regularly rinsing it out in a small bowl of water. Ella's face was flushed and her eyes were closed so that Harker couldn't tell whether she was aware of his return. Taking off his gunbelt and hanging it on the bedpost, he walked over to Mary.

'I thought she was getting better,' he whispered, not wanting to wake Ella if she slept.

'The fever has come up again,' Mary told him in hushed tones. The hotel girl wasn't pretty, but she had a kind, sympathetic smile. 'Have you any calomel?'

Harker shook his head. 'No, will that help?'

'Yes, it gets rid of the poisons in the body.'

He looked down at Ella. The girl's hair was stuck wetly to her head and, as soon as Mary moved the cloth away from her brow, more perspiration began to glisten there.

Harker asked, 'Can I get any of this stuff in Bannon?'

'Yes,' Mary replied, continuing her cooling task. 'Muller, the barber on Main Strip sells it.'

'I'll be back,' Harker said, as he hurried to the door. Remembering Jud

Fielding's warning that men had come out of Lolo Valley looking for him, he added; 'If you have to leave Ella, lock the door.'

* * *

'Harker!'

The sound of Harker's name being called came in through the open window of the hotel waking Ella from a fitful doze. Weak and burning with a fever, she lay still, trying to get her mind to function properly. At first she wasn't sure where she was. Then her senses returned and she heard an angry male voice shout the name again. 'Harker!'

A glance around told her that she was alone in the room, Harker's gunbelt hanging on the bedpost. Twisting on the bed a little, her heart started a panicky thumping as she saw Harker's rifle standing in a corner of the room. He was out on the street unarmed!

Sitting up, Ella had to wait for her spinning head to steady. Standing, she crossed the room with difficulty. At the window she looked down into a street deserted except for two men. One, clad in black and with a revolver in his hand, stood in the centre of the street, calling out Harker's name at fairly regular intervals. Ella couldn't at first see Harker, but then she spotted him. He was concealing himself as best he could in the doorway of a one-storey building that had a flat roof. Unarmed, he was holding a small package in one hand. The shouting gunman was heading in Harker's direction, one slow step at a time.

Going to the corner of the room, Ella caught hold of the rifle with both hands and dragged it to the door. Drained of energy by the effort, she had to lean against the door, panting. Aware that there was no time to lose, she forced herself to move, reaching for the handle of the door. It was locked from the outside.

With tears caused by strain and frustration running down her cheeks, she dragged the rifle to the window. About ten feet below there was a sloping roof leading to a drop of about twelve feet to the ground. Going to the bed, half lying on it for much needed support, she pulled off the sheets and knotted two together. Tying one end to the leg of a wash-stand affixed to the wall close to the window, she tossed out the sheets and watched them drop to the sloping roof. Balancing the rifle on the sill, she clambered out of the window needing to cling to the side as her giddiness increased. Then, with the rifle painfully trapped under one arm, she lowered herself down the rope she had made from the sheets.

It strained every part of her, and when she reached the sloping roof so did she lose control of the rifle. Clinging to the sheets with one hand, she made a sweeping grab with the other to catch the rifle in mid air. Expecting to need to rest, she found that concentrating on climbing down had somehow taken her mind from her illness. What was causing her problems was the drop from the roof to the street below. There was no possibility of even a makeshift rope here. Ella decided that the only thing to do was to slide down to the edge of the roof and try to lower herself as far as she could by her arms, and then let herself drop, hoping for the best.

Sitting, with her legs stretched out facing the street, the rifle cradled on her lap, she let herself slide. Gaining speed, she was approaching the edge at an alarming rate. If there was a way to slow herself, Ella had no time to find it. Clutching the rifle, she shot out over the edge.

For a split second everything seemed to be fine. Ella was suspended in space, sitting comfortably on air. But then she plummeted like a stone. The rough ground was rushing to meet her. Some instinct had her straighten her limbs so that she landed feet first. But it was a jarring landing that slammed the bones together in every single joint of her body. Her left foot buckled under her, the ankle shooting an intense pain right up through the leg. Although she clung to the rifle, the stock hit the ground, and the barrel cracked hard against her head. Ella's last thought as everything went black was that she had failed Harker.

★ ★ ★

The gunman was young. Harker saw that as a bad sign. Not only would Emlyn Rodgers be paying him to do this job, but the young gun would be after the prestige of killing Asa Harker, the man who had outdrawn fast-gun Claude Videll.

Having got the calomel from the barber, Harker had been intent on hurrying back to the hotel with it when the gunman had stepped out of a saloon to call him by name. Unperturbed, Harker had put the medicine in his left hand, leaving his gunhand free as he turned to face the man calling him out.

That was the dreadful moment when he found that there was no gunbelt around his waist. The other man was walking toward him, but the distance between them was still too great for him to see that Harker was unarmed.

Encouraged by seeing Harker run, aware that he was hiding somewhere up ahead, the black-clad gunman had kept up a steady pace as he came along the street. He shouted again. 'Come out, Harker. I'll give you the same chance as you gave Viddel!'

The doorway that Harker was in was deep enough to give him protection, but only until the gunman came fifteen feet or so nearer. Harker looked around, seeking more secure shelter. But there was nothing on his side of the road. Across the street and a little further along were some cattle pens that would provide him with the chance of escape. But he couldn't cross the street without making himself an easy target.

'Harker!'

Close enough to see Harker now,

the gunslinger fired twice. A bullet hit the doorframe on each side of Harker, at head height. Wood was torn away and a long sharp sliver sliced through Harker's right ear. Blood gushed from it down his neck, shoulder and arm.

Out on the street the gunman let his six-shooter drop into his holster, then stood with both hands held a little out from his sides.

'I'm waiting, Harker,' the gunman called tauntingly. 'Start drawing as you come out, and I'll still get you.'

Unable to permit himself the indignity of a plea for mercy, Harker was not prepared to let the gunman know that he was unarmed. He tried to conceive some plan that would permit him to get to the hotel for his gunbelt, but knew that it was hopeless.

'I'll count to three,' the gunslinger shouted.

'*One* . . . '

'*Two* . . . '

Harker heard his first name called, very softly and from above. Dismissing

117

it as some kind of trick his mind was playing under stress, he waited for the gunman's final number to be shouted then heard his name spoken again, and knew that this time there was no mistake.

'Ella?'

'I'm on the roof above you,' Ella whispered, 'and I've got your rifle.'

The reprieve the girl represented sent a surge of energy through him so great it could have made him reckless. Disciplining himself, putting Ella's safety first, he said quietly, 'Listen carefully, Ella. Stay down and bring the rifle straight above me. Hold it horizontally with both hands and let go completely when I say.'

'I'm ready, Asa.'

'Now!'

Catching the rifle as it dropped, Harker took a sideways leap out of the doorway, pre-empting the gunman with a shout of '*Three*!'

Hand going to his holster, the gunman died with a smile on his face as Harker fired his rifle from the hip. The heavy slug caught the gunslinger in the chest, carrying him upwards and backwards for about six paces before he went down heavily on his back to send up a cloud of dust.

6

The trial of the handsome bandit and his beautiful accomplice was a big event in Bannon. In a court-house packed to capacity, the mood of the crowd was that of a theatre audience. Harker, with a front seat beside Henry Keswick, found the lighthearted atmosphere to be offensive. There was a selfishly callous indifference toward the accused. Having spent his adult life in pursuit of, and capturing, wrongdoers. he believed that, whatever their crimes, they deserved respect as human beings. For the townsfolk of Bannon, Ben Whitman and Ruby Malone were a novelty peep-show at a circus. The biggest regret was that no murder was involved, so the town would not be treated to a public hanging.

When the prisoners, both handcuffed and dishevelled, were brought out,

Harker was conscious of Ruby Malone's eyes scanning the crowd until they found him. Seemingly satisfied, she held his gaze for some time. There was a message in her eyes that he was incapable of reading. When she turned away and was sitting downcast, he fretted over missing out on whatever it was she was trying to communicate to him. She looked to be little more than an untidy shadow of the striking woman he had spoken to yesterday. Her magnificent mane of golden hair was dull and unkempt. There was a slump to her shoulders similar to the dejected slouch of a tawdry-looking Ben Whitman. Harker could tell that the people of Bannon were disappointed. Having been led to expect a god and goddess of outlaws, they found themselves looking at two very ordinary desperadoes. At that time Harker could neither believe nor could he understand the drastic change in Ruby Malone.

It had been necessary for him to leave the courageous Ella back at the hotel. Her supreme effort in saving him from the gunslinger had caused her a serious relapse. Harker had called in the town's doctor. With the permission of the hotel, he was paying Mary to nurse her.

Harker still found it difficult to credit what Ella had done for him. Not only had she, though very ill, climbed out of the hotel window with his rifle, falling to the ground, knocking herself out and spraining an ankle in the process, but she had taken a circuitous route through the town to climb up on to the flat roof from behind. Having known many brave people in his time, mostly men, none of them came anywhere near Ella Berry. He owed her his life, and that was something that he would never forget.

When Henry Keswick arrived at the scene of the shooting, Harker had not objected to being arrested. Once the marshal had established from Ella, and some men who had seen the killing from a nearby window, that the shooting had been a fair one, Harker had been released. The dead gunman was identified as Hank Fergus, a wanted man who had evaded the law by living in Lolo Valley.

As they waited now for the proceedings to begin, Keswick complained, 'You've added to my worries since you rode into town, Harker. Even this here trial is down to you.'

'I don't follow you there,' Harker answered, accepting that there was more levity than rancour in the marshal's observations. 'It was you who arrested Whitman and the woman.'

'I don't deny that, but I wouldn't even have heard about them if it weren't for you, Harker!'

Their conversation ended there as Judge Bower made a sweeping entrance into the court. Getting his first sight of Bower, Harker abandoned all hope for Whitman and Ruby Malone. Bower was the youngest judge he had ever seen. Lean and sinewy, he would have resembled a point rider rather than a justice had it not been for a high forehead that completed the face of an intellectual. To Harker, the judge looked like a toughie who could handle just about anything, both inside and outside of a court.

The jury was made up of twelve Bannon men who, despite sitting stiff and uncomfortable in store-bought clothes, had been given an overdose of self-importance by a sense of occasion.

There was nothing remarkable about the entrance of Prosecutor Williams. A small, nervous man, Williams was lopsided by the books that he carried under one arm. He certainly didn't have the look of the successful prosecutor Henry Keswick said he was, but Harker had long ago learned that appearances can be deceptive, and he accepted the town marshal's appraisal as accurate.

It was very different when Colonel C.T. Alexander, every inch a showman, came striding into court. A big man with a body that was still powerful although running to fat, Alexander made an impressive figure with his collar-length silver hair flowing from under a broad-brimmed stetson. His flamboyant entrance was an affront to Judge Bower, but a delight for the crowd. Recognizing Harker as he passed him, Alexander halted, did a military right turn, then saluted smartly as if Harker, who had not served in any army, was his superior officer.

Taking up his position in the courtroom, absorbed in the papers he was studying, Colonel Alexander didn't seem to notice when the prisoners were charged with robbing the banks at Bowbridge and Demsville. Both pleaded not guilty, but that soon looked like being a waste of time when Prosecutor Williams skilfully presented a case that would seem unanswerable. He called G. Joshua Bentley, of the Bowbridge bank, to positively identify the prisoners as the man and woman who had so calmly robbed him. Oliver Nimrod and George G. Cousins, of the

Demsville bank, were also witnesses. They, too, still smarting from having lost money, pointed to Whitman and Malone as the culprits. Williams put forward a damning case, but Colonel Alexander turned everything around when he began the defence.

Walking up and down past an intimidated G. Joshua Bentley who was on the witness stand, he would suddenly turn to ask a question in his southern drawl.

'You are a banker of considerable experience,' he told Bentley, 'and you say that the couple who robbed you did so only because their demeanour and appearance fully satisfied the criteria you set for judging people as being honourable and trustworthy?'

'Yes.'

'These were smart, sophisticated people of substance?'

'Quite so.'

Doing a fast quarter turn, Colonel Alexander shot out his right arm to point a finger at Whitman and Ruby

Malone, shouting a question at Bentley. 'Are you prepared to so describe these poor, bedraggled, humble people who stand accused here?'

'No . . . well, yes . . . that is . . . ' Bentley stammered.

'I should think you would hesitate,' Alexander barracked the witness. 'That sorry-looking man and woman are my clients, and I am mindful of that. But in truth I would not leave a milch cow tethered at the back of the house if they were riding by. Are you seriously telling this court that you saw that pair of ruffians as fine, upstanding citizens?'

Thanks to Colonel C.T. Alexander, G. Joshua Bentley was no longer sure what he was telling the court. Now Harker understood why Whitman and Ruby looked as bad as they did. On this occasion Alexander's craftiness amused him, but there were times previously that Harker had seen a man he had spent months tracking go free as a result of a similar performance by the colonel.

Neither Oliver Nimrod nor George W. Cousins fared any better when it was their turn. Using skilful rhetoric, Alexander made them both appear to be outlandishly stupid. Caught between admitting that they were mistaken about the identity of the prisoners, or confessing that their professionalism was defective, the two bankers chose the face-saving way out by implying that Whitman and Malone were possibly not the man and woman who had robbed them.

'I have another witness, Judge Bower,' a shaken Prosecutor Williams said.

'Why did you not inform the court of this wit — ' the judge began, then fell silent on realizing that Williams had, quite rightly in normal circumstances, relied upon the testimony of the witnesses already called to prove his case. Bower said gruffly, 'Very well.'

The new witness was Tommy Russell, the boy who had seen the window of the First National Bank of Bowbridge shatter by buckshot, Whitman and

Malone coming out of the bank soon afterwards.

Frightened by everything and everybody in the court, the boy walked to the witness stand on legs emaciated either by malnutrition or rickets. Following the lad, the prosecutor came close to putting a fatherly arm around his narrow shoulders. Resisting that urge, Williams spoke coaxingly, patronizingly, to the boy.

'I want you to look over there, Tommy,' Prosecutor Williams pointed in the direction of the prisoners, 'and tell me if you have ever seen that man or that woman before.'

'I know them. They robbed the bank; I saw them!' the boy said, in a loud voice, then he shouted accusingly, coming close to tears as he pointed at Ruby Malone. 'She kicked me!'

Williams gave the jury a triumphant look as Tommy Russell lowered his head and wept quietly. Then the prosecutor stepped back as Colonel Alexander walked up to take the boy's head in both hands and used his thumbs to wipe tears from the lad's cheeks.

'Now, now, Tommy,' the colonel said in gentle tones that were surprising coming from him. 'Crying isn't very Davy Crockett-like, is it? Especially for a brave young chappy like you. You saw a bank being robbed and had the craw to do something about it, didn't you, Tommy?'

The young witness nodded and Alexander went on, 'You saw them taking the money and putting it in a bag. Is that right, son?'

'No, I didn't see nothing like that, sir.' Tommy Russell shook his head.

'Oh dear, that's what I thought you saw. Yet you know that they robbed the bank?'

'I knows that, but I weren't close enough to see what was going on.'

A smug smile creased the colonel's heavy face for a moment. Then he went serious again. 'So you weren't really close enough to see what the robbers looked like.'

Dropping his head, the boy started to cry once more, but Alexander laid a big hand on his shoulder, saying, 'No more crying, Tommy. You have every reason to be proud of yourself. That woman came a lot closer to you, didn't she, and you were very brave. You stood your ground, and got kicked for your troubles. Where did she kick you, Tommy?'

'In the back. She rode on her horse after me, and kicked me,' the boy sobbed, as he remembered his fright and his pain.

Colonel Alexander patted his shoulder sympathetically. 'I just want to make sure that I have this right, son. She was riding after you and kicked you in the back. So you must have been running away. That would mean that you didn't really see the woman, is that right, Tommy?'

'Yes, sir.'

With his case in tatters, a fuming Prosecutor Williams made the mistake of trying to blacken the characters of the accused by referring to the stage-coach robbery. This annoyed Judge Bower, who fixed the prosecutor with a glare.

'Prosecutor Williams,' the judge thundered, 'the prisoners do not stand accused of robbing a Wells Fargo stagecoach. If it is your intention to bring such a charge against them, correctly presented and to include the testimony of witnesses, then you must do so through the proper channels. Will that be your intention?'

'Not at this time, Judge Bower,' Williams replied in an apologetic way. 'I can only cite the dubious courtroom tactics of Colonel C.T. Alexander as the cause of my transgression.'

With his long hair flying wildly, an irate Alexander leapt across the courtroom with an agility that belied both his considerable size and advanced age, to confront a quivering prosecutor.

'As a Southern gentleman, suh, a Confederate colonel who fought at

Wilson Creek and like places,' roared the colonel, 'I will not tolerate being insulted by some Billy Yank with more wind than a bull in green corn time. I invite you, suh, to meet me out on the field where we will settle our differences in a manner suited to men of honour.'

The outlandish prospect of a duel between prosecuting and defending counsel in a court of law terrified Prosecutor Williams, enraged still further an already angry Judge Bower, and caused pandemonium in the public sector of the courtroom. Tommy Russell, who had been standing to one side, forgotten, ran away from the violently arguing adults, probably fearing another kick.

'I will not have this unseemly behaviour!' Judge Bower yelled, adding, 'Town Marshal, do what you can.'

'Everyone stay seated,' Henry Keswick stood to order the crowd, rifle held at a business-like angle across his chest. 'And all of you simmer down.'

'Choose your weapons, suh! If it be the knife, then we shall be tied at our left wrists, by God!' Colonel Alexander shouted across the room at Williams, belligerence in each of his body movements, a threat in every gesture he made.

Keswick had quietened the crowd. Every inch a lawman he stood erect, his oversized nose adding to his proud stance. Using the marshal for protection, Prosecutor Williams went round him to get to the judge.

'Judge Bower,' Williams began, 'in the light of this disruption, I request that court be ad — '

'Judge Bower!' Alexander raised his voice to cut in. 'The fact that the prosecutor got the short end of the horn is no reason for this case to be held over. The testimony of each and every one of the witnesses has totally collapsed. I ask, implore thee, nay, I beseech thee, Judge Bower, suh, to ask the jury to reach a decision right here and now.' He turned to Williams.

'Then, suh, you and me will go to the field with our heads high, two gentlemen of courage putting our lives, our futures, but not our reputations, thanks be to God, in the hands of Nemesis.'

'You, Colonel Alexander' — Judge Bower pointed an angry finger at the defence lawyer — 'you will be meeting Town Marshal Keswick, not some Greek divinity, if you can't get control of yourself.'

Encouraged by this, Prosecutor Williams asked, 'My request for an adjournment, Judge Bower?'

'Request denied,' Judge Bower shouted, above the growing commotion in the courtroom. 'There is no case to answer. The jury is dismissed. The prisoners are free to leave the building.'

This sudden and surprise decision had everyone milling around. Harker tried to fight his way to the door before Whitman and Ruby could get away from him, but they were nearer to the exit than he was. When eventually he got out of the court the pair were nowhere in sight. Henry Keswick came up beside him, a doleful expression on his face.

'Well, I reckon as how that verdict is the one that'll suit you best, Harker,' the marshal commented. 'But them two seem to have skedaddled out of town. You better get after them mighty quick.'

'Can't be done,' a frustrated Harker shook his head. 'I've got a sick girl down at the hotel, Keswick. She needs me right now more than I need to go after them.'

Tucking his rifle under his arm, Keswick took out the makings, rolled a cigarette, then passed the tobacco and papers to Harker. This was a kind of ritual, a bonding that Harker normally avoided. But he liked Henry Keswick, so he did the rolling, passed back the makings, and they both lit up.

'If I were you' — Keswick inhaled deeply before blowing smoke through his oversized nostrils — 'I'd try not to let Wells Fargo know where your priorities lie.'

'I just work for them, Henry. This little girl saved my life.'

'Then I guess you got it about right,' the town marshal nodded in agreement, as Colonel Alexander came striding up as if about to give the order for a regiment to go into action.

'Asa, it's good to see you,' Alexander said, at the top of his booming voice, thrusting out a hand for Harker to shake. Larger than life and twice as noisy, he enquired, 'How do you come to be in these parts?'

'All in the line of duty, Colonel,' Harker replied, shaking the hand and indicating Keswick with a sweep of his other arm. 'This is Henry Keswick, the town marshal.'

'Real pleased to meet you, suh,' Alexander greeted the marshal as Harker studied him, puzzled.

'Seems to me you came a long way for a mighty small reason, Colonel,' Harker remarked, wondering why Alexander had gone to so much trouble for an outlaw of Whitman's low calibre.

The colonel delayed answering as Prosecutor Williams came hesitantly out of the courthouse, his right shoulder pushed up high by the books carried under his arm. Starting in their direction, Williams slowed his pace when he saw Colonel Alexander standing with Harker and the marshal. Williams stopped for a moment, either reluctant or frightened to once again expose himself to the colonel's verbal big guns.

Exchanging a worried glance with Harker, Keswick said warningly, 'I sure hope you don't intend to continue that disagreement of yours out here in the street, Colonel, as I'll have to stop you.'

'What took place in the courtroom was no more than a charade, Marshal,' Alexander chuckled. 'It served its purpose, but it was an act performed on the judiciary stage. I ask you, in all honesty, hand on your heart, would you expect Sarah Bernhardt to continue to be *Camille* when the curtain has been lowered, or Shakespeare to write you a letter so wordy that it tries the patience and damages the morals? No, suh, that was simply a performance, and a damned good one at that, in all modesty.'

Harker understood it all, including the references to the great actress and the renowned writer, and he saw that the less-travelled Keswick got the gist of what the colonel meant.

Williams went past them apprehensively, offering no response to Alexander's friendly, 'A very good day to you, Prosecutor Williams, suh!'

'You were telling me,' Harker jagged the colonel's memory as Williams hurried on his lopsided way, relieved to have got past the colonel unscathed.

'Was I, Asa, was I?' Alexander frowned absently. 'What was I telling you?'

'Why you came here to defend two small-time outlaws.'

'Ah, yes, so I was, so I was. The old mind's slowing down a little, Asa. That's what comes from prolonged exposure to the sound of cannon,' the colonel said in his expressive style. 'It's this way, Asa. Lieutenant Cass Whitman, the uncle of that boy on trial here, was an officer under my command in sad times. In that awesome Fall of '64, when the leaves dropping from the trees could not keep pace with our falling soldiers, we were retreating southward under General Sterling Price. We had been on the last raid of the Confederate army, Asa, and, the Lord help us, were no more than a straggle of tattered grey riders. That was when Cass Whitman, a fine officer who had fought bravely at my side over many years, died. One moment, the man I had come to admire was there before me, whole and as wholesome as one could wish; the next moment, he had been blown into a million tiny pieces by a Ketchum grenade. That is my most poignant memory of the war, suh. What I did for that boy in there was an inadequate token of respect for a very fine officer.'

Though bored by the colonel's verbosity, Harker was pleased to hear this. He had feared that his endeavours to get Ruby Malone to co-operate on the stolen money might be jeopardized if Ben Whitman had connections with powerful people. A battlefield debt, once removed since it was owed to Whitman's uncle, being paid by Colonel C.T. Alexander, was no threat at all to Harker's plans. Once Ella was well enough, then he would be on the trail of Ruby Malone, who would doubtless still be riding with Whitman.

'Your sense of honour does you proud, Colonel,' Harker, tongue in cheek, congratulated the lawyer.

'Altruistic to a fault,' Alexander

complimented himself thoughtfully. 'A veritable fool to myself.' Brightening up, he said, 'Now, you two gentlemen will join me for dinner at the hotel this evening?'

'I appreciate the invite, Colonel,' Henry Keswick politely replied, 'but if me and my rifle ain't patrolling the Main Strip once the lamps are lighted, then this town will blow itself up.'

Recognizing that the marshal's excuse was genuine, and envying him, Harker sought a way out for himself. An evening with Colonel C. T. Alexander would be a punishment rather than a joy.

'I understand, Marshal.' Alexander's fleshy face registered his disappointment. 'It's a pity because I plan it as a celebratory dinner, a chance to toast the freedom of young Whitman and his woman.'

'They will be there?' Harker asked sharply, unable to believe this luck.

'Of course. That is what's behind the

idea,' Alexander answered. 'I trust that you wish to join us, Asa?'

'I'm really looking forward to it,' Harker replied, and he was being completely truthful.

7

Asa Harker was torn between being pleased that Ella had joined them, and worrying about her. He was aware that it was the prospect of seeing Ben Whitman again that made her leave her sickbed. Her ashen face, thinned by illness, she sat happily beside the young outlaw at the hotel table. Despite her illness, Ella had a glow that Harker attributed to Whitman. Ruby Malone, who sat on the far side of Colonel Alexander from Harker, couldn't have failed to notice the young girl's ardent interest in the young outlaw, and that it was reciprocated, yet she seemed unmoved by it. Ruby had returned to being her beautiful self. Elegant, with her golden hair piled high, it was difficult to imagine her riding like an Indian brave, clutching her beloved Henry rifle. Harker, normally completely self-possessed, had discovered at the start of the evening that he was even more vulnerable now to the presence of Ruby Malone than he had been when visiting her in Keswick's cell. It heartened him that he frequently caught her studying him. Ruby looked away as soon as he noticed, but that didn't stop her repeating her observation.

Colonel Alexander ordered what was a lavish meal to those accustomed to a spartan lifestyle. They had turkey, the meat of which was deliciously tender and had a fine nutty flavour, together with collard greens, a Southern vegetable served with bacon.

Harker had learned that Ruby, on the advice of the colonel, had abandoned her intention of retrieving the money in the saddle-bag that was taken from her husband just before he was lynched. She declared that her only interest now was to have the men who had killed her husband caught and punished. Having given the colonel the name of Sheriff

Turps Hallam, she had expressed her willingness, and that of Ben Whitman, to go with Harker to Tascosa and help him round up the gang.

Though he preferred to work alone, Harker couldn't see a way in which he could refuse this offer. Realizing that he shouldn't trust Whitman, Harker did acknowledge that an extra gun would be useful if the outlaw was on his side.

Being aware of Ruby's Henry rifle, Colonel Alexander extolled the 16-shot, breech-loading firearm to Harker, saying, 'I faced Union troops with Henry rifles in the war, by God, suh! Those bucktails would load the damned things in the morning and fire them all day!'

That was a typical Alexander exaggeration, but while Harker appreciated the valuable help a Henry rifle would be, he would never agree to having a woman fight beside him.

'This Hallam is a bad lot, Asa,' Alexander warned as he held up a half-eaten turkey leg and tilted his head to one side to savagely attack it with big teeth. 'You'll need to have a few of your lot back you up.'

'There's only me,' was Harker's simple answer.

'Then, suh, Hallam and his gang will shoot you down like a dog,' the colonel stated emphatically.

'If necessary I'll ask the sheriff for help,' Harker said.

'That's better,' Alexander acknowledged, raising a hand shining with turkey grease. 'You do that, son. Don't take any chances . . . ' He paused for a moment, bemused. Then he said loudly, 'Just a minute! Hallam is the sher — !'

'I know,' Harker kept a straight face.

Ella gave a tinkling little laugh, genuinely amused; Whitman chuckled, and Harker was certain he saw a smile twitch at the desirable lips of Ruby Malone.

'Sorry, Colonel,' he apologized. 'The

humour in that appealed to me.'

'Jest not about such things, for death will not be mocked, suh!' the colonel rebuked Harker. 'Had you been in my command at the battle of Cold Harbor, Asa, you would share my respect for the Grim Reaper. In just eight minutes we lost fifteen hundred, while the Yankee dead totalled seven thousand. Bodies, as thickly laid as possible, covered more than five acres of ground. But this is not the talk of dinner-tables with ladies present. Forgive an old man his bitter reminiscences, my dears. Now, we have done justice to the turkey, so what shall it be: brandy sour, shall we say, eh? Champagne, perhaps? Just state your fancy, for this night my purse is yours.'

Champagne was chosen, and Alexander also ordered sweet potato pie, most of which he consumed because the appetite of the others had been fully satisfied. Recharging the glasses of everyone at the table, the colonel beamed at them all, Ruby and Ella in particular, as he announced, 'By God! I have enjoyed this evening. Pleasant company, beautiful women, magnificent food, and fine liquor. What more could a man want? I can barely restrain myself from standing to propose a toast to General Robert E. Lee!'

'You'd better restrain yourself, Colonel,' a laconic Harker advised.

'No, by God!' Alexander objected. 'I will propose a toast, a revised toast.' He leaned nearer to Ruby. 'I am an observant man, my dear, a trait which I may add has saved my life many a time. But I digress. This evening I have been aware just where your interest lies. So I would ask you, Ella, and young Ben, to lift your glasses with me to toast Ruby and Asa, who I predict will have a great future together.'

Ruby blushed a deep red, and Harker was uncomfortable for her as well as himself. It was Ella who neatly saved the moment by standing up from the table to say, 'I thank you kindly for the dinner, Colonel Alexander. It was most enjoyable. If you will excuse Ben and myself, we are going to take a short stroll before retiring.'

Colonel Alexander and Harker stood as the young couple left the table, with Harker issuing a word of caution. 'Don't go walking too far, Ella. Don't tire yourself.'

'I won't, Asa, I promise,' Ella turned to assure him, a sweet smile on her face.

'If you don't mind, gentlemen,' Ruby Malone said, 'I think I'll go to my room. Goodnight to you both.'

When they were alone, Alexander took out a packet of Turkish Oriental machine-made cigarillos, offering one to Harker. 'I have these sent specially from New York.'

When the women left, the ease of the evening went with them. Harker, a loner, was always on edge when in the company of one other man. There was no way of escaping into himself, nothing to create a diversion.

'You know that I'm not a man

to fool around with words, Asa,' the colonel began, when he and Harker were drawing on the strange-tasting cigarettes, 'and there are two things I must say to you. I'll come direct to the point. In going after Turps Hallam you will be putting yourself in peril. Not only is he a ruthless bandit at the head of a gang of damned renegades, but, until you prove otherwise, he has the law on his side because he is a sheriff. You go against him when he's wearing a star on his chest; that says he can shoot you down with no questions asked.'

Drawing smoke deep into his lungs, looking at his companion through half-closed lids, Harker wryly observed, 'You told me you'd come direct to the point, Colonel. I sure must have missed it.'

'I did indeed make my point, suh,' an indignant colonel replied. 'You will be riding into danger accompanied only by, and please accept that I mean no disrespect to the ladies when I say this, an ailing little whore, a widow on heat, and a youthful, undependable bandit.'

Despite Alexander's prefix that he wasn't being disrespectful, Harker found the colonel's derogatory descriptions of Ella and Ruby to be offensive. Initially angered enough to take up the matter with the older man, Harker decided to let it slide. As soon as Ella was well enough to ride they would be leaving Bannon behind and Colonel C. T. Alexander would be going his own way.

'I'll have the means to deal with Hallam when the time comes,' he said.

'Maybe so, maybe so, Asa, but you need a real fighting man at your side,' Alexander insisted, 'which is why I have decided to shelve my immediate commitments and join you.'

'It's a long ride to Tascosa, Colonel,' Harker cautioned.

'You're suggesting that I'm not able to make the ride!' Alexander's big face flushed with anger. 'By God, suh, your insult would have me invite you out to the field where we would settle our differences, were it not that I have known and respected you for a mighty long time. Had you seen me ride at Gettysburg, suh, scattering those damn Yankees to left and to right, you would not cast these aspersions, suh!'

'Gettysburg was a long time ago, Colonel,' Harker said quietly.

Alexander bristled aggressively. 'Are you saying you don't want me along?'

'I won't keep you from riding with me, Colonel, but if you drop behind, then I'll leave you there.'

'Drop behind you say, suh!' the colonel snorted. 'By God, suh, you'll be eating my dust!'

'You'll have your chance,' Harker nodded, getting up, about to leave when he recalled that Alexander had said he had two subjects to broach. He asked, 'What was the second thing that you wanted to say to me, Colonel?'

Harker witnessed the impossible happening before his eyes. Colonel

C. T. Alexander, the most successful, garrulous, self-promoter of all time, seemed to shrink in size as he took on a sheepishness.

'The thing is, Asa, old friend,' the colonel said in a low tone that didn't seem to belong to him. 'The thing is, that I dashed away to help Lieutenant Cass Whitman's nephew without proper preparation, in a financial sense, that is. It has left me embarrassingly stuck for the odd dollar or two. I was hoping that you might be able to settle up with the hotel for tonight's dinner.'

'Leave it with me,' Harker said flatly. 'Goodnight, Colonel.'

'You're a real gentlemen, suh, a real gentleman.' Alexander rediscovered his old booming voice. 'I'll pay you back, never fear. I'm a man of my word, suh.'

Taking this in, Harker was walking away when the colonel called after him, 'Just one more thing, Asa. I don't think that the funds I brought with me are sufficient to take care of my board here at the hotel.'

'I'll see to it,' Harker said as he walked out.

Up on the first landing he saw Ruby Malone waiting outside the door of his room, a shawl around her shoulders. It was a scene that thrilled him, a woman waiting for her man to come home. What man hadn't at some time dreamt of having a beautiful, dynamic woman like Ruby for a lifetime partner?

'What's the trouble?' Harker asked, metaphorically forcing himself away from her so that he could think clearly to deal with whatever had brought her here.

Running a tongue over dry lips, unintentionally taking his attention away from her answer, she replied, 'When I left the dining-room I went out of the hotel to see that Ella was all right. A man was riding past, Harker. He was one of the men who came to the cabin after Edward.'

'Are you sure?'

'Absolutely certain. I think he was heading for Rosie Diamond's place.'

'What did he look like?' Harker quizzed her.

Ruby thought carefully. 'He was riding a skewbald. He had a floppy-brimmed stetson on his head, and a black moustache that drooped at each end, Mexican fashion. He wore a cloak, with sleeves, some kind of dark colour. Oh, and he was wearing Bluchers.'

'Right,' Harker nodded, hiding from her how pleased he was to have the chance of getting hold of one of the gang before even starting out for Tascosa.

'If you're going after him, can I come with you, Harker?'

'No, go to your room,' Harker replied. 'I'll let you know what happens.'

'I'd like to be there with my Henry,' Ruby Malone said wistfully.

'I know that.' He gave her a brief smile. 'But I want this man alive, not dead.'

★ ★ ★

'You've got yourself a problem with the colonel, Asa,' Henry Keswick remarked, as he and Harker rode up Prospect Hill together. After leaving Ruby, Harker had walked around the town until he had come upon the marshal. Keswick, in his relaxed manner, had just stopped a shooting in a saloon by breaking the jaw of one protagonist with a terrific blow of his huge right hand. That had been enough to sober up the other would-be gunman and send him running.

They moved their horses along at a walking pace. Those going up to the Blue Goose had to come down the same way, so there was no rush. It would be impossible to miss the man Ruby had identified as one of Turps Hallam's gang. A quarter moon was obliging with enough light to recognize the rider from the description she had given.

'I don't see that,' Harker said.

157

'I figure to lose the old windbag somewhere between here and Tascosa.'

'You'll be lucky.'

'It sounds like you know something that I don't, Henry,' a puzzled Harker said.

He could see the marshal give a shake of his head in the moonlight. 'I guess it's just that I see the situation differently,' Keswick explained. 'Seems to me that good old C.T. is more interested in the money in that saddlebag than he is in seeing a crooked sheriff brought to justice.'

When first considering what the town marshal was suggesting, Asa Harker dismissed it. But then Alexander's lack of finances made it seem feasible. Although the colonel had excused it by saying that he had left home hurriedly, it could well be that he was totally without funds.

'Could be he has ambitions that way, Henry,' he conceded, 'but how could he hope to pull it off?'

'Maybe he's arranging the help of

young Ben Whitman, Asa. One favour deserves another in return.'

'If that's the case,' Harker reasoned, 'they'd be trailing me anyway, so I might as well have them with me where I can keep an eye on them.'

In his pessimistic way, the town marshal put the other possibility forward. 'Behind you they'd have to wait for the right moment, but travelling with you they could take a shot at you any time they liked.'

They were at the Blue Goose then, Keswick nodding toward a pale-yellow horse with numerous black patches, tied to the hitching rail.

'I guess that's the skewbald, Asa.'

Dismounting, they hitched their mounts and Harker walked to the skewbald, looking it over. The rifle scabbard was empty, and he said, 'We'll need these, Henry,' as he collected his own rifle.

Two men, both unsteady on their feet, came out of the Blue Goose as Keswick and Harker went in. The latter checked the men out. Neither came anywhere close to the description given him by Ruby.

'What an unexpected pleasure, Marshal,' Rosie Diamond greeted Keswick with forced friendliness, her wary eyes sweeping over Harker, recognizing him. 'Nice to see you again. I always regard it as a compliment to my premises when a client comes back. Now, can I get you both a drink?'

'We ain't making a social visit, Rosie,' Keswick replied, scanning a room in which men were drinking and playing cards, and a couple of girls stood around, bored and idle. A tired-looking pianist could have saved his energy, for nobody was listening to his rendition of '*Little Brown Jug*'.

'I've never known you to do so, Henry Keswick, but I keep on hoping,' Rosie complained.

Middle-aged, she was a plump, matronly woman. Harker had never seen a whore-house owner with her innocuous looks. Most were retired girls themselves, heavily painted in the hope of disguising age lines. In contrast, Rosie Diamond was every man's idea of a mother. Perhaps that was why she was so successful, Harker thought.

'We're going to take a look around out back, Rosie,' Keswick said, his rifle under his arm like a man going hunting.

'I'd rather you didn't, Henry. That sort of thing can ruin business for an awful long time.' Rosie objected in a half-hearted way that said she was resigned to not being able to dissuade the marshal.

'I could ruin it for good, Rosie,' Keswick said ominously, as he and Harker walked away from her. 'I moved you off the Main Strip, but being up here don't put you out of my jurisdiction. Keep that in mind.'

With Keswick leading, he and Harker went through a door into a small hall which had a number of doors leading off. There was a smell of cheap perfume and stale liquor on the air. Behind one of the doors a girl gave a shrill laugh that was as empty as a chorus girl's smile. Starting at the first door, the town marshal held his rifle at the ready and gave a nod for Harker to open the door.

A woman gave a little scream and a man shouted angrily, but the occupants of the room remained unseen, shielded by the door. A calm Keswick ordered, 'Show us your boots, fella.'

'I've got 'em on,' the man in the room muttered.

'Tut, what shocking habits!' a serious-faced marshal joked to Harker, then ordered the man. 'Stick a leg out and show me.'

There was some scrambling inside of the room, then a pair of male legs with sagging, crumpled Levis around the calves, were put on show. There were high-heeled, tooled leather boots on the feet.

'Sorry to have disturbed you.' Keswick made a false apology, and Harker closed the door.

They partly entered three more doors in the same way with similar results. But when Harker eased open the next door they knew their search had ended. Standing on the floor in front of them was a pair of half-boots with an open front laced over a tongue. Out of date now, they were rarely seen. Both Harker and Keswick recognized them as Bluchers; boots named after the Prussian general.

They heard a girl's frightened gasp from inside the room, and a male voice called harshly, 'Who is it?'

'Bannon's town marshal,' Keswick replied. 'Just step out where we can see . . . '

The marshal's words ceased as a shot was fired inside the room and a bullet smashed through a door panel, passing close to Keswick's head. He and Harker pulled back, one each side of the doorway, keeping tight against the wall.

The shot caused doors to open all around them. Girls and their clients, both frightened but for different reasons, peered through narrow openings at Keswick and Harker. Rosie Diamond, with two of her henchmen close behind her, came running in through the door from the outer room.

'Stay inside and close your doors,' Keswick yelled at the girls, then shouted at their boss, 'Go back out, Rosie, and leave this to us.'

Doors were quickly shut, and Rosie Diamond did as she was told. Keswick raised his rifle in one hand. The marshal was telling Harker what he already knew, that it had been a rifle fired at them from within the room. Harker nodded, then used his clenched fist against his chest to mime the beating of a heart, a message to Keswick that he needed to take the man alive.

In the circumstances that would be extremely difficult. All that Keswick could offer him in return was a shrug that said nothing.

8

The door with the shattered panel had been kicked shut from inside. Keswick and Harker could hear the girl in the room sobbing. It was a stand off. They could smash open the door and charge in, blasting away as they went, but that would kill both the man and the girl. To go in cautiously would make them both targets for the rifle the man inside had already shown himself eager to use. Keswick came over to stand beside Harker.

'How do you reckon we can take it from here, Asa?' the marshal enquired in a whisper.

'The rooms have no windows,' said Harker, recalling his visit to Ella, 'so he won't get out that way.'

'It's us getting in, not him getting out, that's got me beat,' Keswick muttered disconsolately. 'How much do they pay you, Asa?'

This was an odd question, particularly in this situation, but Harker answered, 'Three dollars a day.'

'That's a dollar a day more than me, but it still ain't the beatenest amount of money!'

'Are you telling me something, Henry?' Harker asked.

'All I'm saying, Asa, is that you and me could ride way from here right now, and have a right peaceful time, and get more money chasing dogies out on the range.'

'That wouldn't do for either you or me,' Harker said.

'I guess you're right,' Keswick said with a sigh, moving away. 'I've got a brother with the United States Marshal's office, who's been going on at me to become a deputy.'

'What's the pay like?' Harker enquired, aware that he and the town marshal were having this normal conversation not despite the siege of an innocent girl held in a room, but because of it.

'Two dollars a day. Just the same as I'm getting here,' a despairing Keswick replied.

'I guess you won't be going then, Henry,' Harker remarked.

Shaking his head, the town marshal said, 'The only place I'm going right now is to have a word with Rosie.'

Keswick left Harker an unhappy man, and came back even worse. 'That gal in there ain't yet seventeen years of age. She's called Libby, a danged silly name for an unfortunate kid. We ain't got no right to go killing a child just to get back Wells Fargo money.'

Not wanting to harm the girl any more than the town marshal did, Harker's loyalty didn't allow him the luxury of a choice. He told Keswick, 'I've got to do whatever the job requires of me, Henry.'

'I just knew you were going to say that,' the town marshal groaned.

'If you don't like what I say, then you're free to say *adios* and ride off,' Harker said.

'I wouldn't have liked it if you had answered any other way.' Keswick clapped a hand on Harker's shoulder. Then he called, 'Libby?'

'Yes?' the girl called back querulously.

'Can you walk out of that room?' the marshal asked.

This time it was the man who responded. 'No she cain't. She don't do nothing without my say-so.'

It was looking bad, Harker realized. At no time had the man in the room enquired as to why they were after him. Obviously he had a price on his head and was expecting the law, or perhaps bounty hunters, to catch up with him at any time. With probably a death sentence awaiting him, the man holed up in the room had nothing to lose whatever he did to resist capture.

'Let the girl go and we'll talk,' Keswick said.

'The girl stays here,' the man in the room said, adding confidently, 'and I'll do the talking while you out there do the listening.'

'We're listening,' the town marshal said resignedly.

'I'm going to come out with this girl in front of me.' The man began what sounded like a mentally rehearsed speech. 'I don't want there to be no guns in sight, and I want the rest of the girls to walk with me out to my horse. I want a girl at the front, another behind me, and the others walking on each side. You got that?'

'We've got it, and we're moving out,' Keswick replied, as he motioned Harker to go with him to the door leading out of the hall.

Beckoning Rosie Diamond to him, the town marshal explained what she had to do. Four girls, all shaking and looking terrified, went to stand fairly near to the door of the room in which their colleague was being held.

The door of the room opened slowly and cautiously. From where they stood just inside of the outer room, Keswick and Harker saw the girl appear first. She was part black. Her long legs were very thin, and her knees were knocking. The man, with a heavy moustache just as Ruby had described, was tight behind the girl, his arms around her holding a rifle against her front, upright with the muzzle pressed so tightly under her chin that her head was being forced back so that she took the faltering steps of a blind person. The quartet of girls formed up around Libby and the man as they had been instructed. The little group began a strange and slow procession toward the door leading to the main part of the building. The exit to Prospect Hill was at its far end.

'There's a hollow over there,' said Keswick, as he and Harker came out of the Blue Goose. He pointed through the night to a place some fifteen yards away from the door. 'I'll take up a position there, Asa, and you go to the corner of the building. We can both see his horse then.'

It was the skewbald that was Harker's major worry right then. Apart from some other horses, his and Keswick's included, that were a fair distance away along the hitching rail, the yellow horse with its distinctive black patches stood alone. He broached his concern to Keswick.

'He didn't ask for a horse for Libby, Henry.'

'I noticed that,' Keswick said sadly.

Harker put into words the horror that was on both their minds. 'Once he's mounted up he intends to kill her.'

'Probably drag her along with him for some distance first.' The town marshal was glum. 'That way he knows that nobody will risk a shot at him for fear of hitting the child.'

They split up hurriedly then, going to their positions as the door opened and lamplight flooded out into the night. Dispensing with the protection afforded inside the Blue Goose by the four girls, the man brought Libby out alone, heading toward his horse, still hugging her from behind, still with the rifle up against her throat.

Without needing to put it into words, Keswick and Harker had agreed that either would fire when presented with a chance of getting the man without endangering the girl. It wasn't likely to happen, for even a reflex action on the part of the man would blow the girl's head off. Their only hope was to wait until he was up in the saddle.

But the moustachioed man was cleverer than they had anticipated. Harker heard him whisper something to Libby, who untied the reins of his horse from the hitching rail. The girl kept hold of the reins, leading the horse as the man headed her down the hill toward town. With the rifle thrusting her head back, and the man hugging her as he had all along, the couple went slowly but surely away from where Keswick and Harker lay uselessly in wait.

There was no cover on either side of the well-used road down to the town. It was impossible even to start following the man without putting the girl's life on the line.

Coming out of the shadows to join Harker, Keswick said miserably, 'He's beat us, Asa, he's got us real beat.'

* * *

After seeing Ella Berry safely into the hotel, Ben Whitman walked slowly along the Main Strip. A young man who liked to keep life simple and enjoyable, he had become confused by the events of the evening. Ruby Malone's decision to go for vengeance and not the money had altered the immediate future as he'd had it planned. Most bewildering of all, though, were his feelings for Ella Berry. At one time the girl had come into his thoughts occasionally when he wasn't with her, but now she filled his mind. That was a bad thing for a man with ambitions to progress through small robberies into the big time and eventually emulate the James boys or the Youngers.

He viewed going to Tascosa as a waste of his time. Yet he owed his freedom to Colonel Alexander, while he and Ruby Malone had been through enough together for her to expect his support. Then there was the biggest reason of all to go along with Asa Harker, which brought him back to Ella. She was going to Tascosa with them, and was looking to Whitman for proof that he intended to forsake his lawless way of life for her. That sure was asking a lot! The question hammering at Ben Whitman was not whether he could make this sacrifice for Ella, but did he want to.

It was late and the night-life in the saloons on the Main Strip was winding down. Those left inside the saloons would be too drunk to interest him. Whitman needed company as much as he needed a drink. He desperately wanted somebody to talk to. Not to discuss the situation he had got himself into with Ella, but just to talk, to have something to concentrate on, so that his mind could wander freely in search of a solution to his problem.

Without planning it, he found himself walking up Prospect Hill. He wouldn't find Ella at the Blue Goose, but Rosie Diamond would be there, ready to listen and advise. A woman of the world, she had also become quite a friend of his.

Whitman realized that he was doing the right thing in climbing the hill. There was a soothing paleness to the moonlight, and the soft night air relaxed him. As he paced steadily, for it was a taxing hill even for a fit young man, he asked himself if Ella was worth changing everything for. The crucial test was in deciding if he could ride away and leave the girl behind. In his heart of hearts, Ben Whitman knew that he couldn't.

Recognizing that fact increased his problem, and he was so deep in thought that he didn't hear the slow clop of a horse's hoofs until the animal and the figures of a man and a woman came out of the semi-darkness in front of him.

But Whitman was not as startled as the man. Uttering a curse, he moved the girl to one side and levelled a rifle at Whitman. With his difficulties caused by Ella Berry driven from his mind, Ben Whitman found himself staring into the black, menacing muzzle of a Winchester rifle. Over the years he had become something of a fast draw, but Whitman was aware that he would be dead before his right hand reached the butt of his holstered gun.

★ ★ ★

Harker and Keswick leapt forward in a soft-footed run when they saw the man up ahead so startled by something that he took his rifle away from the girl's throat. They went fast down the hill. As they got nearer they recognized Ben Whitman standing as still as a statue under the threat of the rifle that was trained on him. Libby was

176

also motionless, held so by the terror of what she had been through in the past twenty minutes or so. All three were so preoccupied by the new and sudden development of Whitman's arrival, that they didn't notice the approach of Harker and Keswick.

There followed a blur of fast action. Swinging his rifle up as he ran, Harker slammed its stock into the back of the neck of the man who had abducted Libby. Keswick swung past the man to grab Libby, pulling her to the ground in case the man had time to fire the rifle, or a spooked Whitman let loose a shot. The two of them rolled over and over down the hill, the girl screaming at the top of her voice, believing the marshal to be yet another attacker.

The noise and the action going on around it panicked the skewbald, which leapt about, slamming against Harker, knocking him to the ground, before running off uphill.

Recovering quickly, the blow struck him by Harker's rifle only a glancing one, the man with the moustache sat up, clutching his rifle. Harker, winded for a moment after hitting the ground hard, had lost his rifle in the impact. The other man's rifle had him covered, and he could tell from the man's eyes, sense from his facial expression, that he was about to pull the trigger. But Whitman came running up, a .45 in his hand that he was aiming at the man with the rifle.

'*No*, Whitman!' Harker yelled, not wanting the man killed after having gone to all this trouble.

Whitman wasn't listening. The man sitting on the ground had taken his rifle away from Harker and was bringing it round to defend himself against Whitman. But he must have known, just as much as Harker did, that he would never make it in time.

Rolling himself down the slope toward them, Harker straightened himself out. Lying flat on his back, he lashed out with his left foot to kick Whitman's legs from under him, while a kick from his right foot sent the rifle flying from the hands of the other man. Whitman's six-shooter exploded, sending red and yellow flame out into the night, but the bullet went wild.

Keswick came back then. Having calmed the girl he had an arm round her thin waist while holding his rifle trained on the man with the moustache. Getting up from the ground, Harker retrieved his rifle and went to Keswick's side. Whitman was scrambling to his feet, rubbing his knees, asking Harker complainingly, 'Whose side are you on, Harker?'

'My own,' Harker answered, as he reached down to pull the man to his feet.

9

'This'd better be worth getting a man from his bed at four o'clock in the morning,' Judge Bower grumbled as he came into the jailhouse. With a coat thrown on over his nightclothes when Keswick had called for him at a private guest-house, and his hair awry, he had none of the dignity of the courtroom.

'It is, Judge,' Henry Keswick assured him. 'We wanted to catch you before you left town.'

They passed through the office to the iron cage where Harker stood over a prisoner whose blackened eyes were swelling so that they were little more than slits. The man's top lip was so swollen that it jutted out in front of his thick moustache.

'Town?' Bower snorted his disgust. 'This is a madhouse, Marshal, not a dang-blasted town. I haven't had to endure anything like Bannon in a coon's age. In my courtroom I've had some old greyback who's deluded himself into believing he's a Philadelphia lawyer, and finishes up challenging everyone in sight to a duel, and now you've got me out of bed at this unearthly hour.' He stopped to take a look at the battered face of the prisoner. 'What happened to him?'

'Had some kind of fight before we arrested him, Judge,' the town marshal lied.

Louis Cordon, the prisoner, had refused to give even his name when Harker and Keswick had brought him down from Prospect Hill. There was no time to spare, so they'd had to rough him up, to break down his sullen toughness until he was ready to talk to save himself further pain. It was brutal, but they had excused themselves with thoughts of Libby, the young mulatto. Harker had learned enough for him to be ready to leave for Tascosa as soon as possible, whenever Ella was fit enough to take the trail. She wouldn't permit Ben Whitman to go without her, and Colonel Alexander insisted that the young outlaw went with them.

'What have you got him for?' Bower asked.

'Quite a few charges, Judge,' Keswick replied. 'He went loco with a rifle up at the Blue Goose. Tried to take one of the girls away with him.'

'Don't charge the man, give him a medal,' Bower said. 'I'm for any man who'll rid society of a whore or two. Now, Marshal, you have wasted my time. I am way to return to my bed.'

'That's not what I got you here for, Judge,' Keswick explained, needing to placate Bower. He introduced Harker. 'This is Asa Harker, Judge Bower. He's a detective with Wells Fargo.'

'Harker,' Bower said grudgingly, before enquiring of Keswick. 'This is going to lead somewhere, Marshal?'

'Sure thing, Judge. The prisoner, Cordon, was involved in robbing a Wells Fargo office down in Wyoming,'

Keswick said, 'and now he wants to make a deposition about that robbery before you. Of his own free will, of course.'

A sceptical Judge Bower reached out a hand, fingers going tenderly under Louis Cordon's chin, tilting his head back and looking at the blue/black contusions covering the face.

'That doesn't look like 'of his own free will' to me, Marshal.'

With a wide-eyed expression of innocence, Keswick said, 'I confess that I'd be more than inclined to agree with you on that, Judge, be every little bit as suspicious as you are, if it wasn't for the fact that I know how he came to be so beat up.'

'I'll believe you, Marshal,' Bower said, in a way that inferred the opposite. 'I'm going back to my bed. You draw up the deposition and call me again, at a more reasonable hour, and I'll come over for him to sign it.'

'The deposition's all ready for his signature, Judge,' Keswick said, prising Bower. 'If you'll just see the signing done, then that'll be it.'

'Can you write?' Judge Bower asked the prisoner. 'Sign your name?'

Cordon gave a sullen nod, and signed his name. Adding his signature, the date and the location, Judge Bower straightened up and said with a sigh, 'I take it that I can leave you now, Marshal.'

'I'm obliged to you, Judge,' Keswick said with a smile. 'I can assure you that I'll take real good care of you should you ever have occasion to come back to Bannon.'

'Marshal Keswick,' Judge Bower said solemnly, 'I would shoot my damned self rather than ever return to this town. I bid you good night, gentlemen, or more fittingly, good morning.'

When the judge had gone, Keswick passed the signed deposition to Harker. 'There's your proof that Sheriff Hallam robbed your office in Wyoming, Asa. I'll keep Cordon here until you need him, although I guess you'll be settling the issue with gunplay and not in a court of law.'

'Whichever,' Harker said, shaking the marshal by the hand. 'It's been good working with you, Henry.'

Keswick smiled. 'We made a good team. When you've settled this business, why not ride back here, Asa, and you and me'll go together to see my brother. Deputy marshals of the United States. That sure has a good ring to it.'

'That's a tempting offer that I may well take you up on, Henry.'

'No, I doubt it,' Keswick said, a little gloomily. 'I allow that you will have a much more tempting invite from a little lady with long golden hair.'

'Would I do wrong to take that invitation, Henry?' a serious Harker asked.

'That's a question I ain't qualified to answer.' The marshal shook his head. 'You ask me how much easier it is to keep law and order with a Winchester repeater rifle than it was with the old rps single shot lever-action, and I'll sit you down for an hour's lecture. I won't keep you a second telling you what I know about women, Asa.'

'I guess I'm no different to you,' Harker said numbly.

'Now that ain't the truth,' Keswick vehemently protested. 'You're a whole heap different to me, Asa, because I ain't got no golden-haired woman breathing down the back of my neck.'

'Ruby Malone isn't breathing down my neck, Henry.'

'That ain't the way I see it,' the town marshal grinned at Harker. Then he said gruffly, 'Now, get out of here, I've got work to do.'

Harker stood on the street in the early chill of a new day. The town of Bannon hadn't come awake yet. There was an emptiness that seemed to creep into him, filling him with a familiar melancholy. He appreciated the abrupt way in which Keswick had closed the door on their relationship. He wasn't one for goodbyes himself. Every one he had ever said, from Mexico to Utah, had stayed with him to add depth to his darkest times. Looking around him at the buildings that went to make up the town, he was saddened by the thought of leaving. Leaning against the wall of a hardware store, he rolled a cigarette. Lighting it, he inhaled deeply, just once, then walked off toward the hotel and the next stage of his life, whatever that would bring.

* * *

They had eaten bacon and Boston baked beans round a camp-fire and now the torpor of a full stomach was adding itself to the weariness of fatigue. An urge to sleep had silenced even Colonel C.T. Alexander. He lay with his head resting on his saddle, his long silver hair spread out around him, a cigarillo burning itself out as it drooped from slumber-relaxed lips, a warrior of yesteryear, out of condition now, able to fight only the battles that d on in his memory.

Across from them, Ella slept the dreamless sleep of childhood with only her pretty, sunburned features showing out of an enveloping blanket. Allowing the sick girl to start out with them had been a gamble. But it had paid off. Ella was regaining her strength by the minute, and Harker, who had become fond of her, was pleased. He couldn't understand her one ambition, really an obsession, which was to be with Whitman. Undoubtedly handsome and a likeable lad, his character was marred by a potential for lawlessness. It was obvious that Whitman had strong feelings for the girl, but whether or not they would prove sufficient to meet Ella's wishes, Harker had his doubts.

They had camped on a wide, level, grassy area on the south slope of a valley. They were all tired, but Ben Whitman was gripped by restlessness and he climbed to the highest point. Standing with his back to Ruby Malone and Harker, he wrestled with something personal that must have been visible only to him in the sun that was sinking in the west. In the distance the peaks of a range of hills were upthrust against the dimness of twilight. Great clouds of scarlet and gold hung in the sky, and the delicate purple haze of dusk was softening and obscuring the edges of the landscape.

'Poor Ben,' Ruby said softly. 'He is uncertain what he wants, and he hopes to read the answer in that magnificent sky.'

'Perhaps it's there,' Harker suggested, out of his depth in this kind of talk.

As the sun slowly faded away, shadows crept up from the lowlands to surround them as they sat together. The higher peaks still glowed faintly as he reached for Ruby's jacket to put it around her shoulders. With the sun gone from it, the air was cold. Turning her face to Harker she thanked him with a shy smile. The switch from a hard, capable woman to a sweet girl was something that perplexed him.

She shook her head to disagree with Harker's suggestion. 'The questions are everywhere, Asa, but you can never find the answers.'

They had become close since leaving Bannon. An easy rapport set them slightly apart from the others. It seemed natural for Ruby to ride with him during the day, and sleep by his side each night. Ella and Whitman had each other, and the colonel needed only the companionship of his bombastic self. He was happy while he could hear his own booming voice echoing about them.

Now that they were less than a day's ride from Tascosa, Ruby had become insecure. Her conversations with Harker were always resting on questions she didn't like to ask. Aware that she was worrying over what would happen when the business with Turps Hallam had been concluded, he couldn't help her as he never allowed himself to think that far ahead. Guns made the future unpredictable, and it was necessary to concentrate on the job to be done. Turps Hallam would have many guns and the law, ostensibly, on his side.

Glancing over at the sleeping Ella, Ruby mused pensively, 'What of Ella if Ben Whitman leaves her in Tascosa and rides off? What could she do? What would she do?'

'She's managed to get along without Whitman until now,' Harker pointed out, with the uneasy feeling that Ruby was really referring to herself and him rather than Ella and Whitman. Men were much more direct than women, which was something he appreciated. But he acknowledged that it was her diffidence that prevented Ruby from saying what was exactly on her mind.

'That wasn't the same, Asa,' Ruby argued mildly. 'Ella was a different person then. When people come into your life, people who mean something to you, they alter you. I'm a very different woman since I met you.'

It was becoming intimate. An intimacy that made Harker uncomfortable, and which he took great care to divert. Having never met a woman such as Ruby, and not having known himself to have feelings for any other woman the way he had for her, Harker still insisted to himself that he didn't have to make any decisions concerning her. His hope was that maybe once he got used to the alien emotions he was experiencing, he might be in a position to make up his mind. Until such a time, if it ever did come, he intended to keep his distance, give nothing of himself away.

'I feel just about the same as ever,' he told her, to take the heat out of the situation that was building up between them.

'That's because you haven't really thought about it, Asa,' she began, but then, embarrassed by her own boldness, she switched subjects. 'How will you go about things in Tascosa? You can't just arrest a sheriff, can you? Will you have to go to a judge first?'

'I can't trust anyone, Ruby. Any judge I go to might tip off Hallam in advance. What I have to do is get the evidence first, then go find a judge,' Harker explained.

'The saddle-bag full of money is the evidence?' she half enquired, pretty sure of the answer.

'Yes. That man we pulled in at Bannon said it is in the safe in Turps Hallam's office.'

'Do you believe him, Asa?'

'I see no reason not to.'

Ruby looked at him worriedly. 'How will you possibly be able to get into Hallam's safe?'

'I've got a plan,' Harker told her, but didn't expand on that statement.

'You'll be in danger, won't you, great danger?' she asked, fearful for him.

'In my job I'm never far from danger, Ruby.'

Reaching for a blanket, she laid it over her legs, pretending to concentrate on what she was doing, but not fooling him. 'I know that, but this thing with Hallam is out of the ordinary, isn't it?'

'It's likely to be tougher than most,' he conceded, in what was a mammoth understatement. He went on, 'We'd better get some shut-eye now. Ruby. We'll be making an early start in the morning. Goodnight.'

'Goodnight,' she murmured.

Harker settled down in his blanket. Sleep evaded him. He was aware of Whitman returning to bed down beside Ella. The girl murmured something, disturbed by Whitman's movements but not waking up. For a time Harker listened to the profound silence that followed the noise of Whitman settling down. There was a magic in it that was never present in a town even at the deepest hour of the night. An owl cried, faint and bodiless on the still air. He found himself waiting for the answering call, attempting to divert his active mind into lulling trivia. The expected cry came from nearby, mournful and eerie. Then it fell quiet again until a pair of coyotes met in a brief, snarling confrontation that was full of vicious aggression. The anger in the exchange caused Ruby to stir.

'Asa?' she called softly.

'Yes?'

'Whatever happens tomorrow.' She spoke slowly, selecting her words with care. 'I shall always be grateful for this time we have spent together.'

Not knowing what to say in reply, frightened that anything he did say might be misconstrued, he delayed answering. The wrong words might suggest some commitment on his part. Perhaps he did want to offer something that would lead to a permanence between them. Yet he couldn't be sure until the Tascosa business was over and the dust had settled.

'It's meant a lot to me, too,' he said at last.

'Thank you,' Ruby said.

★ ★ ★

They moved out an hour before dawn, when the moon was down but the sun not yet up, the time when the first streaks of red begin to fleck the sky. Riding up ahead, Ben Whitman had been looking forward to having Ella at his side, but Colonel C.T. Alexander had had a quiet word with the girl. As a consequence Ella had dropped back and the colonel, tall in the saddle, his long hair and general appearance belonging to the past, had joined Whitman. Ella, apparently having decided that Ruby and Harker wanted privacy as they rode together, kept to herself.

Unspeaking, Alexander seemed lost in some kind of reverie. He had been uncharacteristically quiet since clambering from his bedroll. With the colonel having remained silent during breakfast, something that Whitman knew the others had noticed though they had made no comment, he was suspicious that the old man was up to something.

Alexander spoke as they topped a rise, having turned to make sure that the others were out of earshot. In keeping with the disconcerting habit he had of uttering aloud a continuation of a conversation that had been going on in his head, he said, 'A man who has put everything into life surely deserves it, wouldn't you agree, son?'

'I ain't quite sure what you're getting at, Colonel,' Whitman replied, unable to shake off a feeling that he wasn't going to like what Alexander was about to come up with.

'I was remarking on the unfairness of life, young Ben,' the colonel said. 'Had I been some goober grabber from Georgia I'd right now be enjoying a fortune gotten through peanut farming. But I gave my all, son. I fought in so many battles that were free-for-all slaughters, that I can't remember one half of them. I went without proper food, had worn-out surgeons dig deep into me to pull bullets out, too tired, too uncaring to even notice the agony they caused. Surgeons with hands dirtier than a dog's snout. Malaria took me to death's door, son, but what has life given me back in return? I'll tell you, Ben, nothing!'

They passed a clump of trees and the ground sloped down to a river so suddenly that the conversation had to be suspended while they eased their horses down sideways to keep a footing in the soft earth. Not that Whitman was sure what he should say when more favourable terrain permitted talk to continue. He hadn't asked for the colonel's life story, and couldn't see what the old man's dissatisfaction with life had to do with him.

'You've sure had it tough, Colonel,' Whitman sympathized, 'and though I sure wish there was, there ain't nothing I can do to help you.'

'That's where you're wrong, son, utterly and completely damned wrong,' Alexander corrected him. 'You, Ben, are in a position to reverse my dire financial state while helping yourself at the same time.'

Whitman's anticipated dread had

become a reality. The colonel who, Whitman acknowledged, had got them off the bank robbery charges, was about to call in the debt. Whatever the old man had in mind, Whitman didn't want to know. He had gained respect for Asa Harker, and would help him regain the Wells Fargo money. Harker had said there would be a reward, and Ben Whitman intended to use whatever money came his way to set up life together with Ella.

'All I'm interested in doing, Colonel, is helping Harker and then riding off to somewhere peaceful with my girl,' Whitman said.

Turning his head once more to check Harker and the two women still couldn't hear, Alexander asked, 'Do you trust this Harker fellow?'

'He's a good man,' Whitman nodded.

'Maybe he is, maybe he isn't.' Colonel Alexander gave a hard chuckle. 'That's a whole heap of money he's going after in Tascosa. I can't put a final figure on it, but I know it's a lot. It would be enough to keep me in luxury for the remainder of my days, as well as giving you and that little girl of your'n a good start in life.'

'Are you saying that we should steal that money, Colonel?' Whitman couldn't believe that the old man was serious.

'No, of course not.' Alexander gave a short laugh. 'Not we, son, but you. I did the last of my fighting at Gettysburg, Ben. Now I want someone like you, young, strong and capable, to do it for me.'

The enormity of what the colonel was asking of him struck Whitman who rode on without speaking. Once he had thrown in his lot with Asa Harker, that was it. He wouldn't be able to bring himself to doublecross the Wells Fargo man. Even if he was driven by desperation to try to do so, Whitman was honest enough to accept that he would have no chance against Harker.

'I wouldn't even know how to begin

to get that money, Colonel,' Whitman set out his excuses in the hope of convincing Alexander. 'If I did try, then I'd be no match for Asa Harker.'

Hoping that would be an end to it, Whitman felt his heart sinking as the old man chuckled in a way that said he pitied his misguided, youthful thinking.

'You have it wrong, son, really wrong.' Colonel Alexander smiled sympathetically at him. 'We just sit back and let Harker get the money, then you, with me and my vast fighting experience gained from the battles of that terrible war behind you, will, in turn, relieve Harker of what is sure to be a fortune, Ben.'

This was a frightening prospect for Whitman. He knew that he must not go through with the colonel's plans, but he already owed him a favour, and was aware that the older man completely dominated him. So powerful was Alexander's hold that Whitman did not have what it would take to refuse to do his bidding.

Reining his horse away from Alexander's, he dropped back until he was riding beside Ella. She looked at his face, concerned for him, wanting to ask what ailed him, but aware that it would be unwise for her to do so.

10

Ben Whitman rode alone and slowly into Tascosa. The town had seen enough of the type he was making himself out to be, a young gunslinger intent on making a name for himself. Tascosa sensed that something was going to happen; was certain of it. The very quiet that hugged the early-evening air, right up to the steep roofs of the town's big log houses, gave warning of it. Another drama was about to be played out with the arrival of a renegade who believed he could take on and beat the whole darn world, but who would learn, too late, that he was mistaken, when the gun of Sheriff Turps Hallam or one of his deputies would end his crazy dream. He had been spotted when still a mile out on the trail. In the utter silence, the oppressiveness, the townsfolk knew to stay clear. The shade of the giant cottonwoods up and down the street was deserted even though the day was hot. The only sign of life apart from the row of horses outside of the Blacksnake Saloon, was a shaggy yellow cur that lay stretched out in the damp shadow pool of a log water trough, its chest rising and falling as it panted hard as a pair of bellows. The long hitching-racks in front of all the other buildings were empty.

Dismounting outside of the saloon, Whitman saw the dog lazily open one eye to watch him tie his horse to the rack. Satisfied that Whitman was no threat to it or its slumbers, the dog squeezed the eye closed and recommenced its regular, tongue-lolling puffing.

Pausing for a moment, Whitman steadied his nerves. He was no coward, but Harker had left him in no doubt of the perils inherent in the role he was to play in the Wells Fargo man's scheme. Harker and the others were outside of town, waiting to enter at nightfall. Care was required because Hallam was likely to recognize Ruby Malone.

'Push it just far enough, but not too far,' Harker had instructed him, but the Wells Fargo man had known, just as Whitman did, that the line between those two things was impossible to define.

Before Whitman had left, Colonel Alexander had furtively whispered that he would be there at the end to help Whitman make his move to secure the money for the two of them. Trying to push this from his mind, Whitman had extracted a promise from Harker that Ella would not be exposed to any danger.

Inside the Blacksnake, the same rigid quiet held sway over the drinkers and gamblers. The long, broad room, with its hard-packed earthen floor and its monstrous hewn-log bar was not crowded. There was strangely no noise, and the men present were like ghost figures under the swirling ribbons of tobacco smoke that hung against the rough, black beams of the ceiling.

Aware that he was being covertly watched by all of them, Whitman was satisfied that his pose as a gunman on the prod had been accepted. Everyone here expected a lot from him, as did Asa Harker. The worrying thing was that the expectations of the two factions were opposed. It was down to him to satisfy them both while not getting killed in the process. Now that he was actually here, and could feel the sullen menace of the place, Whitman doubted that his staying alive was an option.

It caused him extra strain to realize that Harker's plan rested entirely on him. In the next minutes it would be decided whether the Wells Fargo man could retrieve his company's money, and it was all down to Whitman.

He looked around. Some of the men sat drinking at crude tables along the whitewashed wall opposite to the bar. A poker game was going on in a corner with four big-hatted, chapped, booted and spurred cowboys playing for modest stakes. Just ahead of Whitman, a man who had been sitting alone at a table, stood, a cynical smile fixed on his hawkish face. He wasn't a big man, but there was something about the way he held himself that advised caution. The sheriff's badge on his breast didn't shine as brightly as other badges Whitman had seen.

The man glanced casually at an old octagon clock that hung on the wall. A bullet hole high in its cracked dial didn't seem to have affected it as a time-keeper. Eyes coming back to Whitman, he said lazily, in a strange voice that hardly rose above a whisper, 'You're late, kid. They told me you were coming, but you're a slow rider.'

Whitman drew in deep breaths without making it obvious. The crucial time was seconds away. He wasn't here to kill or be killed. His task was to provoke Hallam so that the sheriff would lock him up in Tascosa's jail.

'Are you Turps Hallam?' he asked, his own voice given a bleak sound by the silence in the saloon.

'That's me,' Hallam nodded. 'What's your beef, kid? Have I killed your brother, your father, or your cousin, and you're here for revenge? Or is it just that you want to be the one to outdraw Turps Hallam? I warn you, kid, I'm just not ready to be the notch on some bub's gun.'

Aware of two men on his right, one bulky and with a pugnacious face, the other slender and pale to the point of being insipid, both with deputy sheriff badges on their chests, both wearing gunbelts, Whitman continued to prod Hallam. Before reaching the point of no return, he would change tack and shoot out one of the mirrors behind the bar. That would be enough to get himself arrested.

'In my reckoning, Hallam, we don't have no say in choosing how and when we die,' Whitman pointed out, pleased by the profundity of his comment.

'Now that's where you and me differ, bub,' Turps Hallam said in his whispering way. 'You see. I happen . . . ' Breaking off in mid-sentence, the sheriff went for his gun.

Automatically responding, Whitman slapped leather. To his amazement he was beating Hallam to the draw. He recognized this, and the way fear suddenly dulled the sheriff's eyes, he could tell that Hallam knew it.

Whitman carried on, clearing his holster, aware that he had Hallam and that by shooting the sheriff he would be taken to the jail just as Harker wanted. In fact, by killing Hallam he would save the Wells Fargo man from having to do it.

A change in Hallam's eyes warned Whitman that something was happening. His left hand was about to fan the hammer of his gun when the slight-built deputy took a step forward to bring the barrel of his drawn .45 down on to the wrist of Whitman's gunhand. Pain forced Whitman's fingers open and his gun clattered to the earth floor of the saloon. That was when the big deputy hit him on the jaw. A fist the size of a ham thudded hard against Whitman, who was knocked sideways to crash unconscious to the floor.

★ ★ ★

They rode into town after nightfall. Harker and Ruby were in the lead, with Ella close behind them and Colonel C.T. Alexander trailing at the back. They paced their horses just right so as not to draw any attention to themselves. Harker, who had come into Tascosa earlier on reconnaissance, and while there had wired his employers about Turps Hallam, took them past the Blacksnake Saloon and on along the main street, and then taking a left turn between a saddler's shop and a small wooden church. The church stood directly across the street from the town jail. At the end of a shadowy passageway, they rode to a small yard behind the church and dismounted. Leaving their horses they followed Harker on foot. When he had located and squeakingly opened a door, all four of them entered the church.

'Unfurl the bloodstained banner, I will fall to my knees before the fiery cross to pray for the souls of thousands of dead soldiers who march, march, march through the mud and mire of my sinner's mind,' the colonel intoned, as they were all temporarily disorientated by the murky half-dark inside of the building.

'Save it, Colonel,' Harker said cynically, as he looked around him. Built in hope, the church was crumbling from neglect. Harker had seen its like in other places. Paid for by townsfolk seeking finer things than the harsh, often vulgar realities of frontier life, there were never enough itinerant preachers to make a place of worship worthwhile.

Harker wanted it to be a safe haven for the two women and the colonel while he did what he had to do that night.

He watched as Ruby, thoughtless rather than sacriligious, laid her Henry rifle on an altar that had been fashioned with care and devotion. She leaned back, both elbows resting on the altar, as she peered through the gloom in search of Ella. The girl was there, isolated from them by the state of unhappiness and worry she had been in since Ben Whitman had left for town earlier that day. Ruby opened her mouth to say something to the girl, but, deciding against doing so, stayed quiet.

Drawing his own gun Asa checked it over, then did the same to a Colt Peacemaker concealed inside of his coat. Coming to his side, Ruby placed a hand on his arm. She said nothing, but since that day at the court in Bannon he had become skilled at reading her silent messages. Sometimes there was a magic to it, but on other occasions he felt threatened by the profound intimacy.

'I'll be OK,' he assured her, then raised his voice so that the colonel and Ella could hear. 'All being well I'll be gone no more than half an hour. Stay in here, remain quiet, and don't strike any lights.'

'Take care of Ben, Asa, please!' Ella pleaded.

'I will,' he promised her.

Going to the door with him, Ruby hesitated for a split second, then she kissed him lightly on the lips. Her voice was a husky whisper as she begged him, 'Come back to me.'

This time it was Harker who hesitated. As any man would, he was flattered, his sense of self boosted by having a golden-haired beauty declare an ardent interest in him. But he was also alarmed by the way she had forcibly intruded into his personal domain. It had robbed him of something vital so that he was no longer his own man.

Without a word to her he went out into the night. Moving stealthily, watchfully, he made his way across the street. The front of the sheriff's office was in darkness, but as he made his way to the rear, Harker could see light from at least two oil lamps.

* * *

Cecil Plummer, Whitman's jailer, was a skinny old man with a friendly nature. Despite an abominable headache brought on by the crushing blow from the fist of the deputy sheriff in the saloon, Whitman had played cards with Cecil for some two hours before the oldster had become tired. Cecil had made no concessions, leaving Whitman locked in so that he had to extend his arms through the bars to collect and deal cards. Now the jailer slept, gape-mouthed, stretched out in a wooden armchair so that he was lying rather than sitting.

Nerves strained, expecting Harker to arrive at any time, Whitman jumped when he did hear a scraping sound against the rear wall of his cell.

Knowing what to expect, he stood with one leg on his cot, reaching a hand up to the barred window that was high in the wall. Holding the Peacemaker by the barrel, Harker dangled the handle of the gun in through the bars for Whitman to grip.

Stepping back down on to the floor of the cell, Whitman concealed the weapon inside of his shirt and called to the jailer, 'Hey, Cecil. Could you use the makings?'

'That's mighty civil of you, young fella.' The jailer got up to walk over to Whitman, blinking blearily.

When the old man was at the bars, Whitman held out the makings. As Plummer reached for them, Whitman grabbed him by the belt, pulled out the gun and thrust the muzzle against his lean belly, saying, 'I don't want to hurt you none, Cecil.'

'I sure share them sentiments with you, son,' Cecil Plummer said drily.

'Then let me out of here,' Whitman ordered, as the old man was already reaching for the key. 'If I lock you inside will you stay nice an' peaceful-like?'

'You can rely on it, son.' The old jailer gave a toothless grin. 'This ain't Tombstone, and I sure ain't no Wyatt Earp!'

Giving Plummer a sloppy salute, a farewell wave, Whitman hurried over to the safe. Kneeling beside it, he used a nefariously gained knowledge to open it and reach in for a bulging saddle-bag.

★ ★ ★

'I got it, Asa!'

Having heard the door of the jailhouse open and close, Harker was relieved to hear Whitman's soft call. He came round the corner of the building as he saw the shadowy figure, the saddle-bag over its shoulder, heading his way. Harker's faith in Whitman had paid off. He reached for the heavy saddle-bag.

216

'You did well, Ben,' he congratulated the younger man.

'It was easy as falling off a log,' Whitman said. 'All I had to beat was an old-timer of a jail — !'

A bullet slammed into the wooden wall just behind them. Breaking in on Whitman's sentence, it sent splinters flying in a way that told Harker that the slug had come from a rifle. He and Whitman dived for cover around the corner of the building.

'Listen, you men,' a voice called from out of the darkness, sounding like a whisper even though it was raised to a shout. 'I'm Sheriff Hallam. Step out where I can see you. Place that saddle-bag on the boardwalk, then back slowly away with your hands held high.'

Harker shouted back, 'I'm Asalah Harker, Hallam. I'm with Wells Fargo, and this is their money. The state governor knows about you and the Wyoming robbery, and the lynching of Edward Malone. There's a new sheriff on the way to replace you.'

217

A horse whinnied somewhere down the street. The distant sound somehow brought a reality to the situation. A reality that the suddenness of it had chased away.

'Forget about the new sheriff, Harker,' Hallam chuckled. 'I've got six men all around here with rifles pointing your way, so he ain't ever going to see you or that money. Now, start moving. Do like I said.'

'Maybe he's bluffing,' Whitman whispered.

'Maybe he isn't,' Harker reasoned. 'We'll find out. Keep watching, Asa.'

After saying this, Whitman took a step to his left, away from the building. A watchful Harker, rifle to his shoulder, saw a flash across the street, high up and to the right of the church where Ruby and the other two waited. He fired as he sensed Whitman pull back in, unscathed. There was a grunting sigh, followed by the slithering, scraping sound of a falling body. A muttered curse came from Hallam.

'You got him,' Whitman slapped Harker on the shoulder.

'There's still Hallam and five others,' a laconic Harker reminded him. Then he asked, 'You get that rifle in the sheriff's place?'

'Just borrowed it,' Whitman grinned in the shadows, 'and a box of shells.'

'Sshh!' Harker cautioned. 'There's something happening.'

They soon discovered what it was. Hallam had moved one of his men to their left. He was on street level, and had a direct line of fire on them. The first bullet passed between the heads of Harker and Whitman. There was little chance of the next one missing, and they didn't have time to move out, or anywhere to go to take cover.

They waited for the worst when there came a harsh bark of a rifle from across the street. The man who had fired at them gave a scream of agony that ended in a wet-sounding gurgle. Harker had heard it before. It was the death rattle as blood filled the lungs and the throat as a man died. There was something different about the rifle that had fired, but what it was eluded Harker. It was Whitman who enlightened him.

'Danged if that weren't a Henry rifle that just fired, Asa,' Whitman exclaimed.

Ruby! Aware that they were pinned down, she was joining in the fight. It was a courageous thing to do, but with that single shot she had put herself, Ella, and the colonel in great danger. This was confirmed for Harker by Hallam's hoarse shout.

'That came from the church!' Hallam cried. 'Gregson, Stevens, see to it!'

Able to understand the sheriff's consternation at having a gun unexpectedly behind his positions, Harker recognized that Hallam would need to eliminate the problem without delay. He said to Whitman, 'Cover me, I'm going over to the church.'

It was an impossible instruction, and both Harker and Whitman knew it. To fire repeatedly to afford cover in such a situation depended on knowing where the enemy fire was coming from. In the darkness, Whitman had no idea.

'You'll never make it, Asa,' he warned, but Harker had already left him.

Running in a zig-zag fashion but avoiding setting up a pattern, Harker went across the street with bullets singing in his ears. When the firing became too accurate, he slid to a prone position behind a low wall. Within five seconds he learned two things. One was that he was exposed to a rifle, and the second was that Hallam had lied. The sheriff had more than six men.

Scrambling to his feet, he had no option but to make a dash direct to the church. A bullet plucked at the sleeve of his coat, another burned a groove through the heel of one of his boots. But then he was charging at the church door. It opened and he threw himself in, tossing the heavy saddle-bag he had brought with him to one side, aware of

Ella's anxious face as she slammed the door closed again.

Ruby, her loose hair giving her a wildness that seemed to be mirrored in her eyes, turned to glance at him from her position by the window. She had broken the glass and her trusty Henry rifle rested on the sill. Colonel C.T. Alexander sat on a pew, his head down, as lifeless as a corpse.

'We could use another gun at that window over there, Colonel.' Harker said.

'I buried my will to fight at Gettysburg,' Alexander replied, without looking up.

Ella came up to Harker, asking, 'Is Ben safe, Asa?'

'He needs help,' Harker replied, moving to the window. He guessed that Hallam would not move directly against the church now that he knew there were two rifles inside. That meant that Whitman had become the prime target. They couldn't afford to wait until dawn, yet in the darkness they couldn't place where Hallam's men were positioned.

Nothing was coming their way, but Whitman's position was under heavy fire. Harker asked, 'How do you see it, Ruby?'

'They'll finish Whitman off first,' she said evenly, not breaking her vigil as she studied the night through the window. 'Then they'll have nothing to fear from behind, so they'll come for us.'

'How many do you figure there are, Ruby?'

'You and me both got one,' she replied. 'Seems to me there's five left, not counting Hallam. I can't be sure, but I reckon there's two in the warehouse here beside us, while Hallam and the other three are over there in the courthouse.'

Harker took in this information. The courthouse stood at an angle on the far side of the street, its front providing a direct line of fire at Whitman. Yet to venture from the church meant exposing himself to the rifles next door in the warehouse. He looked around and upwards. Above him was an incomplete wooden floor of an intended loft for the church. It stretched for about half the length of the building.

Searching quickly through the debris lying around on the church floor, Harker found an old sack into which he stuffed rags and some straw he had gathered up. Picking up an old oil lamp that lay on its side, he tipped the contents on to the bundle. He was making his way to a gnarled upright beam that was tight against the wall and reached up to the loft floor, when he came across a can that was full of oil. Pushing the can into the sack, he closed the end with some twine. Making a loop in the twine, he slipped it over one arm and began to climb.

Finding hand and footholds was difficult, but Harker, sometimes feeling certain that he was going to lose his grip on the beam and fall back to the floor, eventually made it to within a few feet of the loft floor. But there the beam became smooth. The rough edge of the floor was some six feet away from him, and three feet higher than he was.

Risking everything, he tried to cling to the beam with one hand as he flung his bundle containing the can up on to the flooring. He saw it land safely before he was falling backwards. Plummeting through the air, he prepared himself for the bone-breaking crunch when he would hit the floor of the church, but he fell across some flimsy pews that splintered under his weight, breaking his fall.

Battered and bruised by the fall, he clambered to his feet. Ella, concern on her face, was running toward him. But he was up and clambering up the beam once more. With every limb and joint hurting, he reached the smooth part. Bracing his body, he launched himself through the air, arms stretched above his head.

For one breathless moment Harker

seemed to be dropping, but then his fingers brushed against the edges of the board floor. Clutching at it, he got a grip, then used the momentum of his body to swing himself upwards. Landing face downwards with a crash that sent dust flying, he got up on to his hands and knees, grabbing the sack and can as he did so. On his feet, he ran to the dividing wall between the church and the warehouse, hoping against hope it wouldn't be solid at that height. He was in luck. It was no more than matchboard and he had no trouble in kicking a hole through it.

As always when action was required, Harker came into his own. He felt good, really alive, as he ran across the upper floor of the warehouse. Ruby had been right. There were two men below, and they fired wildly up through the floorboards as they heard him moving about. Reaching an opening in the floor which had a ladder leading down to below, Harker kept back a little as he tipped the oil from the can over his sack of rags and straw. Igniting it, he narrowly avoided setting fire to himself in the blaze that resulted. Kicking at the flaming bundle, he sent it down the hole. As he ran back the way he had come he heard the floor below explode into an inferno.

Back in the loft of the church, Harker leapt into the air, grabbed the wooden stanchion and went down it as agile as a monkey. Several feet from the ground, he jumped. Landing on his feet, he ran to the vacant window, snatching up his rifle along the way. Ruby already had her Henry at the aim against her shoulder.

Flames were leaping out of the warehouse to light up the night. They didn't have to wait long. First they heard coughing above the roar of the flames, then two men came running out, one behind the other as they headed for the courthouse.

As Ruby squeezed the trigger of her rifle, the man in the lead stopped running. Turning toward her, he brought his rifle up to his hip. But it was merely an instinctive movement. A fraction of a second later he crumpled into a heap on the road. The second man folded over backwards as a bullet from Harker's rifle snapped his spine in two.

'The courthouse!' Ruby shouted to Harker.

Agreeing with a wave of his hand, he picked up the saddle-bag and draped it over his shoulder. Shouting, 'Stay here and stay down, Ella,' he ran out of the door with Ruby at his side.

The side of the courthouse facing them was windowless. Reaching it, they flattened themselves against the wall. Leaning close to Ruby, Harker told her, 'I'll go round the back and come in at the other side. I'll holler when I'm there, and we'll hit the front door together.'

Making his way carefully round the building he came up to the front corner at the other side of the building from Ruby. From the two windows that were on each side of the door, rifles were spitting flame as they fired to keep Whitman pinned down. An occasional shot of defiance came from Whitman.

Amusing himself by thinking how it would please Colonel C.T. Alexander, Harker alerted Ruby by giving a rebel yell: the war cry of Confederate soldiers.

They ran to the courthouse door from opposite directions, both doubled over to stay safely below the windows. The door was closed, and Harker had to stand to kick it open. Whitman must have realized what was happening. He had stopped firing. Side by side, Harker and Ruby went in. A man came out through a doorway on their left. Ready to fight, he brought up his rifle to bear on them, but a bullet from Ruby's Henry ripped through his groin.

Shrieking in pain, the man did a crazy kind of dance before rushing past them out into the night. He only got to the top of the wooden steps that went down into the street. That was where he met Whitman, who swung the stock of his rifle to crush the face of the agonized man.

Whitman was in the hall with Harker and Ruby. Then Harker signalled to him, indicating that there were two men remaining, one in the room to the left, the other to the right.

Stepping through the door on his left, Harker pulled himself quickly back out again. A bullet splintered the door jamb close to his head. He stepped back into the room to blow off the top of the man's skull with a rifle bullet from close range.

Whitman didn't fare so well in the room on the right, taking a bullet through the fleshy part of his upper left arm before he gut-shot his opponent.

As Whitman rejoined Ruby and Harker in the hall, Turps Hallam appeared on the landing above a flight of stairs that was in front of them. Still wearing his sheriff's silver star, he was smiling mirthlessly. The rifle he held at his hip covered all three of them.

'Harker! Whitman!' Ruby spoke their names incisively. 'Leave him! Move away!'

Both men took a half step to the side as the rifles of Ruby and Hallam exploded apparently simultaneously. A shocked Harker reached for Ruby as blood poured from her brow and she fell backwards. With his spare arm he brought his rifle round on Hallam, but was a split second behind Whitman. Neither of them fired. The sheriff had retained his horrible smile as he stood looking down at them. Then he came tumbling noisily down the stairs. Stepping forward to look down at the prone Hallam, Harker saw the dark stain of blood that marked where the bullet from Ruby's Henry rifle had entered his heart.

Freeing herself from Harker's supporting arm, using the back of her hand to wipe away blood from the groove Hallam's bullet had carved across her forehead, Ruby bent and tore the sheriff's badge from his chest.

Walking to the door she threw the silver star out into the night, as hard as she could. Harker understood. She may have stopped loving her husband before he had died, but that didn't deter her from avenging his death.

Then, mopping at the blood that was streaming down her face, she headed back over to the church with Harker and Whitman. The blazing warehouse illuminated the street like daylight, and the flames had begun to lick at the church. It was Ella's shout that warned them something was wrong.

'Ben!' came the girl's terrified cry.

The three of them stopped, part-way across the street and fully exposed in the light of the fire, as Colonel Alexander came out of the church, covering them with the rifle he held.

'Do as I say,' the old Confederate officer ordered. 'Lay your rifles down on the ground. That's it. Now you, Harker, toss that saddle-bag on the ground in front of you.'

Sliding the bag of money from his

shoulder, Harker threw it so that it hit the dust a little way in front of him.

'Right, Ben, pick up the saddle-bag and bring it to me, son,' the colonel said.

'You got it, Colonel,' Whitman gave a happy smile, ignoring the contempt with which Harker and Ruby looked at him.

Taking care not to get between Alexander's rifle and the man and woman it covered, Whitman stooped to pick up the saddle-bag. Ella had come out of the church and stood horrified, a hand over her mouth, as she witnessed Whitman's betrayal of her and the others.

'You sure had me fooled, Whitman,' Harker muttered.

'It's just that I always wanted to be rich,' Whitman smiled, as he hefted the saddle-bag, enjoying the feel of its weight.

But then he spun on his heel fast, drawing his six-shooter as he came round to face Colonel Alexander.

Whitman fired the gun, plugging the old man between the eyes. As the colonel fell forward on to his face, dropping the rifle, Ella ran forward into the arms of Whitman, who was passing the saddle-bag to Harker.

'I guess I've got all I want from life here, Asa,' Ben Whitman smiled. He looked at Ruby, who stood stoically, wiping the blood from her face with a pocket she had torn from her jacket, obviously expecting something from Harker. 'You've done well for yourself, Asa. That sure is one special woman you've got there.'

Not answering, Harker had a battle raging inside of himself as he tried to make the hardest decision in his life. Conscious of Ruby covertly watching him, he was aware that few men ever met such a woman in a lifetime, and it would be sheer insanity to reject her. But the thrill he had recently experienced in the fight against Hallam and his men was something that he couldn't do without in the future. He walked slowly toward the alleyway that led to the back of the church.

'Where you going, Asa?' a puzzled Whitman, his arm still around his girl's shoulders, called after him.

Turning, Harker looked at Ruby. With her long golden hair falling around her shoulders, glinting in the light of the flames that dramatically lit her blood-streaked but lovely face, she looked like a woman of times long past who would fight bravely beside her cave-man mate. The impact she had on him left Harker undecided for a moment before he answered Whitman.

'I'm going to fetch my horse,' he said slowly, adding as he turned away, 'I've got to see a man in Bannon about becoming a United States Marshal.'

Other titles in the
Linford Western Library

THE CROOKED SHERIFF
John Dyson

Black Pete Bowen quit Texas with a burning hatred of men who try to take the law into their own hands. But he discovers that things aren't much different in the silver mountains of Arizona.

THEY'LL HANG BILLY
FOR SURE:
Larry & Stretch
Marshall Grover

Billy Reese, the West's most notorious desperado, was to stand trial. From all compass points came the curious and the greedy, the riff-raff of the frontier. Suddenly, a crazed killer was on the loose — but the Texas Trouble-Shooters were there, girding their loins for action.

RIDERS OF RIFLE RANGE
Wade Hamilton

Veterinarian Jeff Jones did not like open warfare — but it was there on Scrub Pine grass. When he diagnosed a sick bull on the Endicott ranch as having the contagious blackleg disease, he got involved in the warfare — whether he liked it or not!

BEAR PAW
Nevada Carter

Austin Dailey traded two cows to a pair of Indians for a bay horse, which subsequently disappeared. Tracks led to a secret hideout of fugitive Indians — and cattle thieves. Indians and stockmen co-operated against the rustlers. But it was Pale Woman who acted as interpreter between her people and the rangemen.

THE WEST WITCH
Lance Howard

Detective Quinton Hilcrest journeys west, seeking the Black Hood Bandits' lost fortune. Within hours of arriving in Hags Bend, he is fighting for his life, ensnared with a beautiful outcast the town claims is a witch! Can he save the young woman from the angry mob?

GUNS OF THE PONY EXPRESS
T. M. Dolan

Rich Zennor joined the Pony Express venture at the start, as second-in-command to tough Denning Hartman. But Zennor had the problems of Hartman believing that they had crossed trails in the past, and the fact that he was strongly attached to Hartman's Indian girl, Conchita.

BLACK JO OF THE PECOS
Jeff Blaine

Nobody knew where Black Josephine Callard came from or whither she returned. Deputy U.S. Marshal Frank Haggard would have to exercise all his cunning and ability to stay alive before he could defeat her highly successful gang and solve the mystery.

RIDE FOR YOUR LIFE
Johnny Mack Bride

They rode west, hoping for a new start. Then they met another broken-down casualty of war, and he had a plan that might deliver them from despair. But the only men who would attempt it would be the truly brave — or the desperate. They were both.

THE NIGHTHAWK
Charles Burnham

While John Baxter sat looking at the ruin that arsonists had made of his log house, a stranger rode into the yard. Baxter and Walt Showalter partnered up and re-built the house. But when it was dynamited, they struck back — and all hell broke loose.

MAVERICK PREACHER
M. Duggan

Clay Purnell was hopeful that his posting to Capra would be peaceable enough. However, on his very first day in town he rode into trouble. Although loath to use his .45, Clay found he had little choice — and his likeness to a notorious bank robber didn't help either!

SIXGUN SHOWDOWN
Art Flynn

After years as a lawman elsewhere, Dan Herrick returned to his old Arizona stamping ground to find that nesters were being driven from their homesteads by ruthless ranchers. Before putting away his gun once and for all, Dan forced a bloody and decisive showdown.

RIDE LIKE THE DEVIL!
Sam Gort

Ben Trunch arrived back on the Big T only to find that land-grabbing was in progress. He confronted Luke Fletcher, saloon-keeper and town boss, with what was happening, and was immediately forced to ride for his life. But he got the chance to put it all right in the end.

SLOW WOLF AND DAN FOX:
Larry & Stretch
Marshall Grover

The deck was stacked against an innocent man. Larry Valentine played detective, and his investigation propelled the Texas Trouble-Shooters into a gun-blazing fight to the finish.

BRANAGAN'S LAW
Alan Irwin

To Angus Flint, the valley was his domain and he didn't want any new settlers. But Texas Ranger Jim Branagan had other ideas. Could he put an end to Flint's tyranny for good?

THE DEVIL RODE A PINTO
Bret Rey

When a settler is cut to ribbons in a frenzied attack, Texas Ranger Sam Buck learns that the killer is Rufus Berry, known as The Devil. Sam stiffens his resolve to kill or capture Berry and break up his gang.

THE DEATH MAN
Lee F. Gregson
The hardest of men went in fear of Ford, the bounty hunter, who had earned the name 'The Death Man'. Yet even Ford was not infallible — when he killed the wrong man, he found that he was being sought himself by the feared Frank Ambler.

LEAD LANGUAGE
Gene Tuttle
After Blaze Colton and Ricky Rawlings have delivered a train load of cows from Arizona to San Francisco, they become involved in a load of trouble and find themselves on the run!

A DOLLAR FROM THE STAGE
Bill Morrison
Young saddle-tramp Len Finch stumbled into a web of murder, lawlessness, intrigue and evil ambition. In the end, he put his life on the line for the folks that he cared about.

BRAND 2: HARDCASE
Neil Hunter

When Ben Wyatt and his gang hold up the bank in Adobe, Wyatt is captured. Judge Rice asks Jason Brand, an ex-U.S. Marshal, to take up the silver star. Wyatt is in the cells, his men close by, and Brand is the only man to get Adobe out of real trouble . . .

THE GUNMAN AND THE ACTRESS
Chap O'Keefe

To be paid a heap of money just for protecting a fancy French actress and her troupe of players didn't seem that difficult — but Joshua Dillard hadn't banked on the charms of the actress, and the fact that someone didn't want him even to reach the town . . .

HE RODE WITH QUANTRILL
Terry Murphy

Following the break-up of Quantrill's Raiders, both Jesse James and Mel Becher head their own gang. A decade later, their paths cross again when, unknowingly, they plan to rob the same bank — leading to a violent confrontation between Becher and James.

THE CLOVERLEAF CATTLE COMPANY
Lauran Paine

Bessie Thomas believed in miracles, and her husband, Jawn Henry, did not. But after finding a murdered settler and his woman, and running down the renegades responsible, Jawn Henry would have time to reflect. He and Bessie had never had children. Miracles evidently did happen.

COOGAN'S QUEST
J. P. Weston

Coogan came down from Wyoming on the trail of a man he had vowed to kill — Red Sheene, known as The Butcher. It was the kidnap of Marian De Quincey that gave Coogan his chance — but he was to need help from an unexpected quarter to avoid losing his own life.

DEATH COMES TO ROCK SPRINGS
Steven Gray

Jarrod Kilkline is in trouble with the army, the law, and a bounty hunter. Fleeing from capture, he rescues Brian Tyler, who has been left for dead by the three Jackson brothers. But when the Jacksons reappear on the scene, will Jarrod side with them or with the law in the final showdown?

GHOST TOWN
J. D. Kincaid

A snowstorm drove a motley collection of individuals to seek shelter in the ghost town of Silver Seam. When violence erupted, Kentuckian gunfighter Jack Stone needed all his deadly skills to secure his and an Indian girl's survival.

INCIDENT AT
LAUGHING WATER CREEK
Harry Jay Thorn

All Kate Decker wants is to run her cattle along Laughing Water Creek. But Leland MacShane and Dave Winters want the whole valley to themselves, and they've hired an army of gunhawks to back their play. Then Frank Corcoran rides right into the middle of it . . .

THE BLUE-BELLY SERGEANT
Elliot Conway

After his discharge from the Union army, veteran Sergeant Harvey Kane hoped to settle down to a peaceful life. But when he took sides with a Texas cattle outfit in their fight against redlegs and reb-haters, he found that his killing days were far from over.

BLACK CANYON
Frank Scarman

All those who had robbed the train between Warbeck and Gaspard were now dead, including Jack Chandler, believed to be the only one who had known where the money was hidden. But someone else did know, and now, years later, waited for the chance to lift it . . .

LOWRY'S REVENGE
Ron Watkins
Frank Lowry's chances of avenging the murder of his wife by Sol Wesley are slim indeed. Frank has never fired a Colt revolver in anger, and he is up against the powerful Wesley family . . .

THE BLACK MARSHAL
John Dyson
Six-guns blazing, The Black Marshal rides into the Indian Nations intent upon imposing some law and order after his own family has been killed by desperadoes. Who can he trust? Only Judge Colt can decide.

KILLER'S HARVEST
Vic J. Hanson
A money man and a law deputy were murdered and a girl taken hostage by four badmen who went on the run. But they failed to reckon on veteran gunfighter Jay Lessiter, or on Goldie Santono's bandidos.

GUN-TOTING DRIFTER
Al Joyson

When John Gelder's ranch foreman is murdered, and Gelder is later forced to flee his own ranch, Deputy Sheriff Ben Winters is convinced that the new foreman, Jason Kenricks, holds the key to the mystery. But who is behind Kendricks? And why?

THE LAST RIDE
John Hunt

When horses were taken from the stage company's corralyard during a night raid. Cody Southwood, the town's sheriff, rounded up some townsmen and went after the thieves. They were to learn that people aren't always what they seem — and that a man's best friend is a loaded gun.